FRONT ROYAL

A Novel

Jim Bennett

RIVERFLOW BOOKS

Front Royal: ***A Novel***

Published by **Riverflow Books** riverflow.com

ISBN: 979-8-9956957-0-7

Cover design and art by the author

Printed in the United States of America

First Edition

PART I

THE FIRST SIGNS

The Discovery

In the spring of '61, when the Shenandoah River rose up out of its banks and flooded half the low-lying homes under muddy water, the people of Front Royal, Virginia did what they had always done in times of trouble — they gathered themselves together like kin.

Front Royal in those days was the kind of place that seemed to sit a little outside of time, tucked between the soft shoulders of the Blue Ridge and the long, quiet sweep of the Shenandoah Valley. At the northern entrance to the Skyline Drive, the town carried the easy rhythm of a community that had learned to live with the seasons; planting, tending, harvesting, and resting in their turn.

The Viscose plant stood at the edge of town like a great humming heart, its long brick buildings and tall stacks rising above the river mist. It was the largest rayon mill in the world then, and nearly every family had someone who worked behind its doors. The plant's whistle marked the hours more faithfully than any clock tower could have, and folks set their days by its call.

People here were close-knit and self-sufficient, bound together by shared work, shared history, and the quiet understanding that neighbors were as necessary as rain. Outsiders were regarded with a polite but steady wariness — not out of meanness, but because the town had always relied on its own. Still, for those who belonged, or came to belong, Front Royal was as fine a place as any to grow up: safe, familiar, and stitched through with the kind of everyday goodness that rarely made the papers but shaped a life all the same.

Families whose houses had been flooded were taken in without hesitation, spare bedrooms opened and quilts shaken out as naturally as breathing. The river had taken its share, as rivers will, but the town answered back with casseroles, strong coffee, and the steady comfort of neighbors who knew one another by name.

By the time the waters receded, the Methodist church basement was stacked high with boxes and bundles for a rummage sale meant to help the families who'd lost the most. Folks brought what they could: a winter coat grown too small, a set of dishes missing a plate or two, a stack of books whose pages still smelled faintly of the homes they'd come from. There was a kind of hopeful bustle in the air — the kind that rises when people decide, quietly and without fuss, to take care of their own.

By the second week of May, the Methodist church basement had taken on the look and feel of a small, good-natured storm. Boxes were stacked in every corner, card tables sagged under the weight of donated goods, and the air carried the mingled scents of coffee, damp cardboard, and the lemon oil Mrs. Talford used on the folding chairs each spring. The Shenandoah flood had left its mark on the town, but the people of Front

Royal were answering back in the only way they knew — by showing up, pitching in, and bringing whatever they could spare.

Terry Miller had volunteered to lend a hand at the rummage sale for the early shift, his flattop haircut catching the light each time he bent over the stack of donations. Slim and of average height, he blended easily into any room—although he hadn't even turned thirty yet, a lot of people in town called him ol' Terry—but he moved with the quiet steadiness of someone who'd grown up doing this sort of neighborly work.

The basement door swung open with a thump of elbow against wood, and in came Jeanie Sonnett, nudging it wider with her shoulder. Two cardboard boxes were stacked in her arms, and her two boys trailed behind her like mismatched ducklings. Jeanie (pretty, red-haired, and not far from forty) still carried the bright, buoyant energy of the cheerleader and homecoming queen she'd once been, the one who married the high-school football captain and somehow kept that same spark through years of motherhood.

"Where do I put these?" she called, her voice warm but already frayed at the edges.

"Just set them down anywhere along that wall. Here, let me help you," Terry said, stepping forward to take the top box before it toppled. Her grateful smile flashed, quick and familiar.

Jake, the older boy (twelve but small enough to pass for ten) hovered near a stack of books and magazines. Skinny, light-brown hair with a hint of red, and a shy way of holding himself, he reached toward a book before his mother even finished lowering her boxes.

"Boys, don't touch any of this stuff," Jeanie warned, brushing a loose strand from her forehead.

"But Mom," Jake said, eyes brightening, "Here's a drawing pad – looks brand new."

"You can look after the sale," she said firmly. "Right now we're helping other people."

Emmett, ten and dark-haired like his father, had already wriggled away from the task at hand. Full of energy, always in motion, he'd discovered a box of costume jewelry and was holding a beaded necklace up to the light as if it were pirate treasure.

"Can I have this one?"

"No, you may not," Jeanie said, plucking it from his hands with practiced speed. "Put that back before you break it."

Terry hid a smile. He'd known the Sonnett boys since they were toddlers, and they hadn't changed much; Jake thoughtful and hesitant, Emmett a sparkler on two legs, and Jeanie forever trying to keep the two currents from colliding.

She straightened up, exhaling. "I swear, these two are going to be the end of me. I told them we were coming here to help, and all they heard was 'treasure hunt.'"

"Well," Terry said, "in a place like this, you never know what you'll find."

She laughed, shaking her head. "Don't encourage them."

"What's Bill up to today?" Terry asked.

She gave a small, amused huff. "Helping his dad clean out the garage. They'll be bringing things here once they decide what's actually worth donating and what's just… well, Sonnett men clutter."

Terry grinned. "We'll take whatever they find. Even the questionable stuff."

"I'm sure you will," she said, shaking her head fondly. "Those two could fill this whole basement if they're not careful."

They continued chatting for a moment about the flood, about the families staying with relatives, about how the church ladies had already baked enough pies to feed half the county. The boys drifted from table to table, touching everything they weren't supposed to, while their mother kept one eye on them and the other on Terry.

A heavy-set man wearing an old fedora hat came in hunched over, struggling to carry what looked like an old sewing machine in a case.

"Hi. Need a hand there?" Terry asked.

"Nope. I'll set this down right here. Gosh, that thing's heavy," the man said as he straightened up and began to look around. "Looks like you got some good stuff for the sale."

Terry reached into one of the cardboard boxes for the next thing that needed dusting and a price tag. His hand closed around a framed, faded picture—a print of an old door standing just ajar, a blade of bright light cutting into a shadowed room. He held it out at arm's length, studying the way the light seemed to spill forward as if it meant to step into the world.

He turned the frame over. The hanging wire was frayed to threads, and a long rip ran down the backing paper. When he lifted the loose edge to see how badly it was torn, something thin and folded slipped free and fluttered to the floor.

Terry leaned down, picked it up, and unfolded it. It was old. A tiny piece of one corner broke off in his hands.

It was a drawing in pencil and ink with delicate, looping lines that curled like vines, with faded curving strokes running through the center forming a bow. At first glance it looked like a child's attempt at a map, but the longer Terry studied it, the more it seemed like something else entirely. A pattern of some kind with mysterious markings.

In the upper corners, written in a neat, elegant script, were two sets of initials, C.N. and A.M.

Terry turned the paper over, then back again, feeling a small tug of curiosity. The bustle of the basement continued around him, Mrs. Sonnett calling for Emmett to put down a candlestick, Jake asking if he could get the sketch book, but for a moment Terry felt as though the room had gone still.

There was something special about the drawing, something that said it didn't belong in a rummage-sale.

"Hey. Whatcha got there?" the man in the fedora hat asked as he peered over Terry's shoulder….

"An old drawing of some sort."

"Looks like a board game," the man commented as he turned away toward something more interesting on the other side of the room.

Terry checked the box again and saw the name written in fading pencil: *Marigold.*

Everybody in Front Royal knew that name. The place sat just outside the town limits off High Knob Road, a once-grand property now sagging into the weeds, its windows boarded, its chimneys beginning to crumble. Folks said it had been standing since before the Revolution. Some said it was haunted. Haunted or not, it was a house full of secrets, heirlooms, and the kind of mystery that clung to a place long after the people were gone.

Terry studied the looping lines of the drawing, the faint X marks, the careful, deliberate hand behind them. The Marigold estate had been full of old things — *real* old things.

Terry refolded it carefully and slipped it gently into his shirt pocket.

As Mrs. Sonnett gathered her boys and prepared to leave, Jake lingered near the table where books were stacked. He was leafing through the pages of the drawing pad.

"Mom," he said, "I want to get this drawing pad. You know I'm always asking you for paper to draw on. And I've got my own money from my paper route."

Mrs. Sonnett let out a breath that was half exasperation, half affection. "Jake, we're here to help other people, not to shop."

"But I *earned* it," he said, standing his ground in that earnest way only a twelve-year-old can. "And it's only one dollar."

She hesitated, then nodded. "All right. But pay Mrs. Talford for it properly. And don't drop it."

Jake grinned, handed over his dollar, and tucked the pad under his arm as proudly as if it were a prize he'd won at the county fair. A moment later, the Sonnetts headed up the basement steps and out into the bright morning, Jake holding onto his valuable purchase with both hands. Emmett skipping ahead in search of whatever adventure might come next.

Terry watched them go, unaware that the small decision Jake had just made would circle back into his own life before long.

Something of Value

By midmorning the church basement had grown warm with the press of bodies and the hum of conversation. Terry brushed the dust from his hands.

His shift was over, and he wanted to pay Mrs. Talford for the drawing he had found, but she was busy helping others. He left two one-dollar bills in her cash box with a slip of paper with his name on it paper-clipped to the bills.

With the folded drawing safely inside his shirt pocket he stepped out into the bright sunlight. The air held that clean, washed scent that comes after a rain — as though the flood waters, having made their mischief, had decided to leave the world a little brighter on its way back home.

Across the street at 24 West Main, the Front Royal Post Office sat square and solid, its brick walls the color of baked clay. Terry had received a notice the day before about a package waiting for him, and since he was already in town, he figured he might as well pick it up.

Inside, the post office was quiet. The ceiling fans turned lazily overhead, stirring the warm air but not doing much to cool it. Phil Jenkins, the clerk at the window, was working his way through a stack of envelopes with the steady rhythm of a man who'd been doing it for decades. Tap on the ink pad, thunk on the envelope. Tap-thunk. Tap-thunk. The old hand stamper moved in his grip like a well-oiled machine, each strike punctuating the quiet post office like a metronome set to "small-town business as usual."

He looked up mid-stamp, his sandy eyebrows lifting. A grin spread across his narrow, foxlike face—half welcome, half the anticipation of fresh news.

"Well now, Terry Miller," he said, setting the stamper down with a final thunk. "You're out early for a Saturday."

Phil had that alert, bird-on-a-branch posture that suggested he was always listening, always collecting. Folks said he could sort gossip faster than he sorted mail, and he never denied it. In fact, he seemed to consider it part of the job description.

"Rummage sale at the church," Terry replied. "They've got me sorting through boxes from the Marigold place."

"That old house?" Phil shook his head. "Betcha there's some stories in those walls."

Terry slid the yellow pickup slip across the counter. "Got a package notice yesterday."

Phil took the slip, disappeared into the back area, and returned with a small brown parcel tied neatly with string and marked fragile—Glass. He set it on the counter but didn't push it forward just yet. With no one else waiting in line, he leaned his elbows on the worn wooden ledge, settling in for a chat.

"That would be the compass I ordered," said Terry referring to the parcel, "from Edmund Scientific."

"Great catalogue. We get lots of things from them coming through this post office," Phil said.

Then he suddenly shifted the subject.

"You hear they're talking about building a new post office?" he said. "Bigger one. The problem's finding a location."

Terry nodded. "Heard something about that. This one's been here since before the war."

"Before *both* wars," Phil said with a chuckle. "She's held up, though. I'll miss her if they tear her down."

There was a comfortable pause — the kind that comes easily between people who've known each other most of their lives. Terry reached into his pocket and gently unfolded the drawing he'd found.

"Take a look at this," he said, smoothing it on the counter.

Phil adjusted his glasses and bent over the paper. "Well now… what do you make of that?"

"Found it behind the backing of an old picture frame," Terry said. "Looked like a map at first, but I'm not so sure."

Phil studied the looping lines, the curved stroke, the initials in the corners. "Could be a pattern for needlework," he said. "See all those Xs. My grandmother used to draw designs like this for her cross stitch."

"That could be," Terry said. "But the curved lines threw me."

Phil shook his finger at the paper as if emphasizing a point to an old friend. "This could be really valuable. A lot of this antique stuff is – especially old documents. I say you ought to show this to Laura Virginia Hale. You know she's got half the county's history in her head. Lives just down the Street — two blocks over."

Terry nodded. "Yup. I know the house."

"Or," Phil added, "you could show it to Mrs. Norton at the library. She's good with old papers. Knows how to date things, too."

Terry folded the drawing carefully and slipped it back into his pocket. "I might do that."

Phil finally nudged the package toward him. "Whatever that paper is, it's got a story behind it. Things like that don't hide themselves for no reason."

Terry thanked him, stepped back into the sunlight, and stood for a moment on the post office steps. The town moved around him in its familiar, unhurried way — cars rolling past, a dog trotting along the sidewalk, the distant sound of a train whistle drifting from the tracks.

He touched the folded paper in his pocket.

Whatever story it held, it felt as though it had just begun to stir.

Most folks in Front Royal would tell you that if you wanted the truth about anything older than your grandparents, you went to Laura Virginia Hale. It was Miss Hale, after all, who kept alive the town's favorite tale about its name — how a British captain drilling his men in the Revolution had barked the order to "Front the royal oak," a great tree that once stood near the center of town. It was a story people preferred to the harsher old name, *Helltown*, earned back when the place was rowdier and full of brawling and drink.

Terry walked the two blocks down Lee Street, the parcel in his hand and the folded drawing resting in his shirt pocket. The houses here were older, their porches deep and shaded, their yards edged with lilacs and iris. He passed Mrs. Talford's place, where a wind chime made from old spoons tinkled softly in the breeze, and then the small white house with green shutters where Laura Virginia Hale lived.

He climbed the steps and knocked gently on the screen door.

It was not Miss Hale who answered, but her companion and caretaker, Mrs. Edith Pruett, a sturdy woman in her sixties with kind eyes and a no-nonsense manner. She wiped her hands on her apron and smiled when she saw Terry.

"Well, Terry Miller," she said. "You're out early for a Saturday."

"Morning, Mrs. Pruett. I was hoping to speak with Miss Hale, if she's up for company."

"She's always up for company," Mrs. Pruett said, stepping aside. "Come on in. She's in the front room."

The house smelled faintly of lavender and old books. Sunlight filtered through lace curtains, casting soft patterns on the polished floor. In the front room, Laura Virginia Hale sat in her wheelchair near the window, her thin hands resting lightly on a small lap desk. Her legs were covered with a neatly folded quilt, and a long wooden stick — smooth from years of use — lay across the desk, ready for typing or turning pages.

Her face, framed by soft white curls, had the dignified calm of someone long accustomed to being both observed and consulted. The high cheekbones, the steady gaze behind wire-rimmed glasses, the hint of a smile that suggested she already knew more than you were about to tell her

Her body was frail, her arms drawn close to her sides, the result of polio as a child, but her eyes were bright and alert, full of the quiet intelligence that had made her the town's unofficial historian for decades.

"Terry," she said, her voice soft but steady. "How good to see you."

He stepped closer, careful not to crowd her. "Good morning, Miss Hale. I hope I'm not interrupting."

"Not at all," she said. "Edith was just reading me the obituaries. A grim business, but it keeps me informed."

Mrs. Pruett snorted gently. "You'd think she was checking to see if she made the list."

Miss Hale smiled, a small, wry curve of her lips. "One must stay current."

Terry reached into his pocket and unfolded the drawing. "I found something this morning at the church rummage sale. Phil Jenkins at the post office thought you might know what it is."

Mrs. Pruett took the paper from him and held it where Miss Hale could see. Miss Hale leaned forward slightly, studying the delicate lines with a concentration that seemed to draw the room into stillness.

After a moment, she spoke.

"This is definitely a sampler design," she said. "Nineteenth century, I'd say. The kind young women drew for themselves before stitching them onto linen."

"Samplers were how girls learned their stitches back then — little practice pieces that showed their letters, borders, and patience. The curved vines here would have been quite challenging."

She nodded toward the curved line running through the center. "That flourish may have been inspired by the Shenandoah River. Many girls used familiar shapes in their designs. All those X's in the design are typical of a sampler."

Her gaze moved to the corner. "And these initials… C.N. and A.M."

She fell quiet, her eyes narrowing slightly as she searched her memory. Terry waited, knowing better than to rush her.

Finally she said, "These were often made to commemorate a wedding — or the hope of one. A girl would stitch her initials, sometimes her sweetheart's as well, into a sampler to mark the beginning of a new life."

Mrs. Pruett adjusted the paper so the light fell more clearly on it. "Looks like fine work," she said. "Whoever drew this had a steady hand."

Miss Hale nodded. "Better times," she murmured. "When a young woman's hopes could be folded into cloth and kept safe."

She looked up at Terry, her eyes sharp and searching. "Where did you say you found this?"

"Behind the backing of an old picture frame," he said. "In a box from the Marigold place."

Miss Hale considered this, her expression thoughtful. "There's a story behind this, Terry. I can feel it. And stories have a way of finding their way home."

"Do you think it's valuable?" Terry asked hopefully.

Miss Hale paused, then answered, "It really could be. I suggest you might take it to Mrs. Norton at the library. She has a good eye for old papers. But bring it back to me when you've learned more."

Terry folded the drawing carefully and slipped it back into his pocket. "You're the second person who has suggested that I talk to Mrs. Norton. I'll come back and tell you what she says, Miss Hale. I promise."

He said his goodbyes and stepped back onto the porch, the scent of lilacs drifted on the breeze, and he felt again that quiet tug — the sense that something long forgotten had begun to stir.

As he walked back toward the post office, Terry glanced to his left and up the hill toward Warren County High School, its brick façade catching the late-morning sun. That magnificent building with its white columns had stood through its share of hard seasons—none harder than the recent, uneasy days of school integration—and yet it still rose above the town with a kind of quiet dignity, as if to remind folks that a community could bend without breaking.

Hard to believe he'd graduated from there almost eleven years ago. He'd been an average student with average grades, the kind of boy teachers liked because he showed up, did the work, and never caused trouble. Perfect attendance. "Most Reliable," his senior yearbook had called him — a title that had felt more like a polite consolation than an honor.

His older brother and sister had gone off to college and built lives somewhere beyond the Blue Ridge. His brother was a science teacher, his sister a nurse down in Roanoke. Terry had stayed in Front Royal. He'd gone straight to the plant, worked his way up to foreman, saved what he could, bowled on Thursdays, hunted in the fall. But most of all he loved the river—fishing, canoeing, or just drifting along with the current on a warm, sunny day.

He'd dated here and there, but nothing had ever taken root.

He'd once imagined a wife, a couple of kids, a house of his own — but at twenty-nine, that dream felt like something he'd set down somewhere and forgotten to pick back up.

He was especially good with his hands, good with machines, good at keeping things running, but lately he'd felt a restlessness he couldn't name — a quiet desire to do something that mattered, something that might lift not just himself but the town he'd always called home.

Now, with this old drawing tucked against his chest, he felt the faintest spark of possibility – a possibility that he wouldn't let slide by this time, as if the past had reached out and brushed his sleeve.

He'd read enough stories to know that valuable pieces sometimes turned up in the unlikeliest places. Coins hidden in walls. Letters tucked behind cracked mirrors. Artwork forgotten behind cheap frames.

Things that changed a person's luck.

And for the first time in a long while, Terry felt the faint, inspiring flicker of possibility.

He wasn't a man who gambled or chased after pipe dreams. He'd never been that kind. But as he thought of the fragile paper, a thought rose in him with quiet insistence.

Maybe this is something valuable.

Maybe this is my chance to do something that matters.

A truth he rarely admitted even to himself flickered through him now, uninvited and undeniable:

I'm tired of feeling ordinary.

He hurried back to his '40 Ford pickup with its dark blue paint faded by years of sun and river weather, parked at the curb across from the post office. He started the ignition, made a sharp U-turn in front of the Catholic Church, and headed east on Main Street. His plan was to drop off a pair of his old boots at Kuser's Shoe Shop to be resoled and then head straight to the library to see the librarian.

The Librarian

After leaving the rummage sale, the Sonnetts were halfway across the church parking lot when Jake shifted the large drawing pad to his other arm and cleared his throat.

"Mom," he said, "could you drop me off at the library on the way home? I finished *While the Clock Ticked* last night, and I want to check out another Hardy Boys mystery. And I'd like to look at the art books too."

Mrs. Sonnett paused beside the car, fishing for her keys in her large bulging purse. "Jake, you know you can't check out another book until you return the first one."

"I brought it with me," Jake said quickly, patting his jacket pocket with a small, triumphant smile. "I'm prepared."

Before she could answer, Emmett piped up from the back seat, already bouncing with anticipation. "If jake's going to the library, I want to go to Compton's! Tommy said they got some new model airplanes!"

Mrs. Sonnett closed her eyes for a moment — the brief, silent prayer of a mother trying to satisfy two children with entirely different dreams. She looked from Jake's earnest face to the drawing pad tucked under his arm, then to Emmett's hopeful grin.

"All right," she said at last. "We'll stop at the library first. Jake can run in, return his book, and get another. Then we'll go to Compton's. But no fussing, and no running off. Neither of you is too old for a spanking!"

Both boys knew full well that their mother's warning was not an idle threat.

Jake nodded solemnly. "And you don't have to wait for me," he added. "I can walk home. It's only four blocks."

"Closer to six," his mother said, giving him a look that balanced caution with trust. "But all right. Come straight home after the library."

"Yes, ma'am. I will," Jake promised.

He set the drawing pad carefully on the back seat opposite his brother and took his place in the front passenger seat. As they headed for the library on Chester Street, Emmett kicked his heels against the seat in excitement, already imagining the new model airplanes at Compton's — a young boy's paradise.

None of them knew — not Jake with his book tucked in his pocket, not Emmett with his restless hopes, not even their mother with her mind on errands — that the quiet stop at the library would brush up against a story far older than any of them, a story waiting patiently for someone to notice its loose threads.

Samuel's Library sat partway up Chester Street, in a white two-story house with black shutters and a small columned porch that made it look more like someone's home than a public building. It had been a residence once, before Dr. Samuels bought it and gifted it to the town, and it still carried that feeling — a place where you might expect to smell supper on the stove or hear a radio playing softly in the next room.

Jake's mother pulled to the curb in front of the iron fence that edged the small front yard.

"All right, Jake," she said. "Run in, return your book, and get another. Then walk straight home. No detours."

"I will," Jake said. He patted his jacket pocket where *While the Clock Ticked* rested. "See you at home."

Emmett leaned forward from the back seat. "Hurry up so we can go to Compton's!"

Jake grinned, glanced back to be sure his drawing pad was lying safely on the seat, then closed the car door gently just as Emmett scrambled over the seat backs into the passenger side. He watched them pull away before turning toward the library and stepping up onto the porch.

Inside, the air was cool and faintly scented with old paper and furniture polish. The front hall had been turned into a small entry area, with a narrow table for returned books and a bulletin board tacked with notices about story hour and civic meetings. To the left, what had once been a parlor now held rows of bookcases; to the right, another room had been lined with shelves and a few sturdy tables for reading.

Behind a modest wooden desk near the center of the front room sat Mrs. Eleanor Norton, Front Royal's first librarian. To Jake, she always seemed tall—taller than any librarian ought to be—with a kind of upright, purposeful posture that made her look even more imposing. Her white hair was neatly arranged, not a strand out of place, and her wire-rimmed glasses rested low on her nose as she scanned a ledger with the brisk focus of someone who ran the library like a well-tuned clock.

When she saw Jake, her face brightened into the warm, infectious smile he'd come to expect, the one that softened all that businesslike efficiency and made him feel, just for a moment, like he was her favorite reader in the whole town.

"Well, if it isn't Jake Sonnett," she said. "I was wondering when you'd be back."

Jake stepped up to the desk and pulled the Hardy Boys book from his pocket. "I finished *While the Clock Ticked* last night," he said. "It was really good."

"I thought it might be," Mrs. Norton replied, taking the book and checking it in with practiced ease. "You never let one sit too long."

She reached down to a small stack beside her chair and lifted a fresh volume, its jacket still crisp. "I set this aside for you — *The Secret of Skull Mountain.* It came in yesterday, and I said to myself, 'That one's for Jake.'"

His eyes widened. "Thanks, Mrs. Norton!"

"And," she added, lowering her voice just a little, "we've a new art book as well. Lots of color plates. I thought of you the moment I saw it."

She rose, moved with care to a nearby shelf, and returned with a large, handsome volume. The cover showed a painter's palette and brushes, bright with oils. She laid it gently on the desk.

Jake ran his fingers over the cover. "Can I check out both?"

"You may," she said. "As long as you promise to carry them carefully. That art book is heavier than it looks."

"I will," he said, solemn as a pledge.

He hesitated. "Mrs. Norton… I'm thinking about entering that art contest they announced at school. The one with the fifty-dollar prize."

Her eyebrows lifted with interest. "Are you now?"

Jake nodded, though not quite as confidently as before. "I'm trying to get ideas. But… well… I'll be competing against kids a lot older than me. Some of them are in high school." He lowered his voice. "I'm kind of worried."

Mrs. Norton's smile softened into something steadier, more knowing. "Jake Sonnett, talent doesn't check birth certificates. And courage doesn't either." She tapped the art book gently. "You keep looking, keep studying, keep painting. Ideas have a way of finding people who are ready for them."

She paused, studying him with that perceptive, librarian's gaze. "And Jake — I never told you how much I enjoyed seeing your artwork in the local artists' show last month. Several of our patrons mentioned it too. You brought something special into this place."

Jake didn't answer. His eyes had gone distant, unfocused, as if he were looking at something far beyond the library walls.

Mrs. Norton tilted her head. "Jake? Are you all right?"

He blinked, coming back to himself. "Yes, ma'am. I guess I was… daydreaming."

She stamped the cards, slipped them into their pockets, and handed the books across.

"Enjoy them, Jake. And keep painting. The world needs more young artists."

"Thank you, Mrs. Norton."

He felt a quiet warmth at that, like someone had lit a small lamp inside him. Balancing the books carefully in his arms, he stepped toward the door.

Just as he reached for the door, it swung inward. Jake stepped back quickly, and there stood Terry Miller, framed in the doorway, a folded paper still tucked in his shirt pocket.

"Well now," Terry said, breaking into a broad, easy smile, "if it isn't young Jake Sonnett. Looks like we're running into each other all over town today."

Jake blinked in surprise, then grinned. "Hi, Mr. Miller."

Terry nodded toward the books Jake was carrying. "Got yourself some good reading, I see."

"Yes, sir. A new Hardy Boys book. And an art book."

"Fine choices," Terry said. "Always liked seeing a boy with books under his arm."

For a brief moment they stood there, the older man stepping aside, the younger easing past him, each carrying something that would matter in its own way. Terry with a folded scrap he didn't yet understand. Jake with books full of bright, open worlds.

"Enjoy your reading," Terry said as his parting words.

"I will," Jake replied, tightening his grip on the books.

And with that, their paths crossed and parted — a quiet, ordinary moment that neither realized was the second small stitch in a story already beginning to pull them toward the same unfolding mystery.

On his way home, Jake ducked into the Royal Dairy. He fed a nickel into the gum machine by the entrance, turned the chrome handle, and caught the bright red gum ball as it rattled down the chute. A moment later he stepped back outside, chewing happily, the sweet bubble-gum taste filling his mouth.

What a great day this has been so far, he thought as he headed home, the books and the promise of new ideas tucked safely under his arm.

The Letter

Terry Miller stepped into the library with the folded paper still tucked safely in his shirt pocket, though "safely" was a generous word. The thing was old — older than anyone he knew — and the corner that had broken off earlier still troubled him. He kept touching the pocket as if to reassure himself it was still there.

"Well, Terry Miller," Mrs. Norton said, her smile widening. "Seeing the Sonnett boy twice in one day. That must mean something."

She gave a small, wry shrug. "Now, I'm not one to claim everything happens for a reason… but if I *did* believe such things, I'd say that kind of timing usually has a purpose."

Terry chuckled. "Maybe it does. And actually… there's something I'd be grateful for you to look at, if you've got a minute."

"For you, I've got two," she said, motioning him closer.

Terry eased the folded sheet from his pocket as though it were something living, something that might bruise if handled too roughly. He spread it on the desk. Mrs. Norton's expression changed at once — a soft, deliberate attentiveness.

"My goodness," she breathed. "This is old. Where in the world did you come across it.?

"It slipped out from behind a picture frame," Terry said. "I bought it at the rummage sale this morning. The backing on one of the frames was torn, and this fell out. It came from the old Marigold estate. At first glance, I thought it was a map, but now I'm thinking it might be a design for a sampler."

Mrs. Norton adjusted her bifocals and bent over the fragile page. The hand-drawn pattern unfurled across the desk — vines curling like quiet thoughts, tiny X's marching in neat rows, and a faint border that hinted at a wedding or an engagement long forgotten. She leaned closer.

"Two sets of initials, if indeed they are initials," she murmured. "C.N. and A.M."

Terry nodded. "That's what caught my eye. If it *is* a sampler design, maybe it was meant to mark a marriage."

Mrs. Norton hesitated, her fingers resting lightly on the desk. "You might call it coincidence," she said, "but I have something I'd like to show you. It may be connected to this drawing."

She opened a drawer and brought out a small letter, its edges feathered with age, the ink still steady and sure.

"I found this last week," she said. "It was inside a donated book — also from the Marigold estate. No envelope, but look here. It's addressed to 'Dearest Alethea'… and signed 'Lovingly yours, Charles.' Alethea could be A.M., and Charles might be C.N."

Terry let out a low whistle. "Well now… that's something."

"It is," she agreed. "I believe the letter and your drawing belong together."

"And exactly what does it say?"

Before she could answer, a middle-aged woman appeared from the back room, holding two well-worn Zane Grey novels. Mrs. Norton glanced up.

"Found something, Becky?"

"I think Carl hasn't read these," the woman said, fanning the books in her hand. "He calls them 'westrins.' Seems being a police officer doesn't give him enough excitement — he's got to have his 'westrins!'"

Mrs. Norton chuckled and checked out the books with practiced ease. "Tell Carl I said he ought to take a vacation if he wants real excitement."

"Oh, he'd just take a book with him," Becky said, waving as she headed for the door.

When the room had settled again, Mrs. Norton turned back to Terry. "Now, where were we?"

Terry nodded toward the letter. "You were about to read it."

Mrs. Norton unfolded the letter with the same care Terry had shown the drawing. Her voice softened as she read:

"'Dearest Alethea, Since my visit a week ago you have been on my mind constantly. I have been thinking about the all too brief time we spent together. I hope the war will be over soon so we can be together without the interruption of my being ordered to fight in this conflict. That is my beautiful dream, my dear. In the meantime, I look forward to hearing from you. Lovingly yours, Charles.'"

Terry smiled, a little wistfully. "A short love note."

"It certainly is a love note," Mrs. Norton said. "There's no date on either of these, but one thing is certain: both pieces are quite old and brittle. They won't stand much handling. If you plan to show this drawing around, you ought to have a copy made."

"That's what I was thinking," Terry said. "But I can't draw a straight line, and I don't know who—"

Mrs. Norton's smile returned, warm and sure. "I do. Jake Sonnett. That boy has a steady hand and an artist's eye. He could make a faithful copy without harming the original."

Terry blinked. "Jake? The boy who just walked out of here."

"The very one," she said. "He's got more talent than he realizes. And he's careful. That matters. Last month, I had two of his paintings on exhibit here with the local artists' show. Did you see it?"

"'Fraid I didn't."

Terry looked down at the fragile paper again, the looping initials like whispers from another century.

"Well," he said slowly, "maybe this is exactly the sort of thing a young artist ought to practice his skills on."

"I think so too," Mrs. Norton said.

Terry thanked her and slipped his drawing back into his pocket. He had just turned toward the door when Mrs. Norton added, almost as an afterthought:

"Oh, one more thing, Terry. I don't believe that's a sampler design at all. I think your first impression was right. It's a map."

Terry stopped with his hand still on the doorknob. "A map?" he said, turning back toward her. "What makes you say that?"

Mrs. Norton gestured toward his pocket. "Samplers follow counted stitches—neat and predictable. Yours doesn't. It wanders, like a river or a boundary line. And those Xs? On a sampler they'd be evenly spaced. These look like markers. It's either a map or an illustration. I'm fairly sure of it."

The Heartbeat of The Town

On Saturday mornings, Main Street carried the pulse of Front Royal the way a river carries its current — steady, familiar, and full of small eddies where people paused to talk. Cars were parked bumper to bumper along both sides, tight as train cars. If you were lucky enough to find a space, you took it without complaint, even if it meant walking half a block. Merchants swept their thresholds, children tugged at sleeves, and neighbors greeted one another as if the whole town were one extended family gathering for the weekly reunion.

Jeanie Sonnett eased her station wagon into a narrow spot in front of Kibler's Furniture Store, the bumper just shy of the fire hydrant. Before she even turned off the ignition, Emmett had scooted forward on the bench seat, ready to spring out the moment she opened her door.

"Compton's first?" he asked, hope bright in his voice.

Jeanie gave him a look over the top of her sunglasses. "We talked about this, Emmett. Mama has errands. Drapery swatches at Weaver's, bathing suits for you and your brother at Coffman-Fisher's, cosmetics at Newberry's, and a payment at Bill's Sporting Goods. If you fuss, we go home. No airplane."

"I won't fuss," he said quickly, though his feet were already bouncing.

They stepped out into the warm bustle of Main Street. Across the way, the Pitt's Park Theater marquee announced *Rio Bravo* and the faint smell of popcorn drifted from the Murphy Theater next to Church Street. Weaver's Department Store had a new display of spring dresses in the window, the mannequins stiff and hopeful in their Sunday best.

Jeanie took Emmett's hand and steered him toward Newberry's. "Just a few things," she said.

Inside, the lunch counter was already busy — farmers in overalls, teenagers sharing a milkshake, Mrs. Smith reading the *Warren Sentinel* with her coffee. Jeanie found her cosmetics and a spool of thread, while Emmett hovered near the toy aisle, eyeing a rack of rubber balls.

"Not here," she reminded him gently. "Compton's."

Back outside, they passed Coverstone's Watch Repair, tucked like a secret door beside Newberry's. A delivery boy from Pomeroy's hurried past with a crate of apples.

"Jeanie! Jeanie Sonnett!"

Clara Whitlow waved from across the street, two shopping bags in hand. She made a careful dash between cars and arrived slightly out of breath.

"Well, good morning," Jeanie said. "You're loaded down."

"Easter dresses for the girls," Clara sighed. "And a new hinge for the screen door. Ramsey's has birdfeeders stacked to the ceiling — looks like a carnival in there."

Her eyes dropped to Emmett. "And what's this young man up to today?"

"Going to Compton's," Emmett said proudly. "Mama said I could get a model airplane."

"As long as he behaves," Jeanie added.

Clara laughed. "That's a tall order."

They chatted a moment about the weather and the new clerk at Citizens Bank. Then Clara leaned in, lowering her voice the way people do when they're about to share something half true and twice interesting.

"Have you heard about the Marigold place?" she whispered. "I hear they're going to tear it down. Build a community center."

Jeanie blinked. "Tearing it down? That old house?"

"That's what folks are saying. Good riddance, some of them think. And you know how people talk — they say the last of the family, that old woman who lived there, was a witch. Kept to herself. Lived to be over a hundred. Never came to town except to buy kerosene and thread."

Jeanie's expression sharpened. "That's awful, Clara. She wasn't a witch. She was just an old woman living alone. My mother knew her. Used to take her soup in the winters. The Marigold woman was shy, not strange."

Clara shifted her bags, a little embarrassed but unwilling to surrender the thrill of the rumor. "Well, you know how people are. They don't like what they can't understand."

"They don't have to tear the place down," Jeanie said. "It's part of the town's history. Seems like everything old is being pushed aside these days."

Clara gave a small, resigned shrug. "Progress, they call it. New roads, new stores, new everything. Folks want modern. They don't want creaky old houses with drafty windows."

"Maybe," Jeanie said, "but once it's gone, it's gone. You can't build history back again."

Clara sighed, her earlier excitement dimming. "I suppose that's true. Still — people say the place gave them the shivers, you know. Kids wouldn't even walk past it on Halloween."

"Kids scare themselves," Jeanie said gently. "Adults should know better."

Clara nodded, chastened but still curious. "Well, whatever they're doing up there, it's starting soon. Trucks, surveyors, men with clipboards. Something's coming."

She gave Jeanie's arm a quick squeeze. "You didn't hear it from me."

And with that, she hurried off toward her car.

Emmett asked, "Are you mad at her?"

"No, I'm not mad at her, son. I just hate it when I hear about old things being torn down. I'll be old one day, and I wouldn't like it if they tore me down."

"I'll protect you, Mom."

"I bet you will. You and Daddy and Jake are my three musketeers."

They strolled down the block to Weaver's. Inside, the air was cool and smelled faintly of cedar and fabric sizing. Bolts of cloth stood in neat rows like soldiers at attention.

"Morning, Jeanie," called Mrs. Striker from behind the drapery counter. "You here for more of that rose print?"

"Thinking about it," Jeanie said. "Bill wants the living room brighter."

"Well, prewash the fabric or you'll be sorry," Mrs. Striker advised. "And give it a double hem."

Jeanie smiled. "That's why I come to you."

Emmett wandered toward the men's hats, trying on a trilby hat that slid down over his eyes. Mrs. Striker laughed. "Looks like we've got a real comedian."

"Emmett," Jeanie warned, "put that back."

They left Weaver's with a swatch tucked into Jeanie's purse and crossed to Ann's Cake Box. The bell jingled as they entered, and a warm cloud of sugar and yeast greeted them.

"Two dozen doughnut holes," Jeanie said, "and please share."

Mr. Henshaw winked. "I'll put in a few extra."

Back outside, powdered sugar dusted Emmett's chin like early snow.

Next came Coffman-Fisher's, where Jeanie found bathing suits for the boys, and then Bill's Sporting Goods, a narrow shop smelling of leather and linseed oil. Jeanie knelt to Emmett's level before they went in.

"Remember — Daddy's birthday. This is a secret."

Emmett nodded solemnly.

Inside, Bill Coffman greeted them. "Morning, Jeanie. That layaway pole's still in the back. Want to put a little more on it?"

"Yes, please," she said quietly. "And keep it hush-hush."

"My lips are sealed."

While Jeanie counted out a few bills, Emmett stood in front of the pocketknife case, his breath fogging the glass.

"Mama," he whispered, "Daddy's gonna like that pole, isn't he?"

"He surely is," she said, smoothing his hair. "But not a word."

They stepped back into the sunlight and could hear the sound of the fire siren calling the local volunteer firemen to a fire. A familiar sound.

Finally, they reached Compton's Toy Store.

The shop smelled of cardboard and rubber balls, and the shelves were lined with model kits — airplanes, ships, cars in bright boxes. Emmett's eyes widened.

"There it is!" he whispered, spotting the P-51 Mustang on the top shelf.

"Ask Mr. Compton to get it down for you," Jeanie said.

While Emmett hurried off, Jeanie took a moment to breathe. Main Street had a way of doing that — reminding her of the town's steady heartbeat, its familiar faces, its dependable rhythm. Everything she needed was here, all within a few blocks. It was a comfort she didn't take for granted.

Mr. Compton rang up the model airplane, and Emmett clutched the bag like a treasure.

"Thank you, Mama," he said, his earlier impatience forgotten.

"You earned it," she replied.

They stepped back into the flow of Saturday shoppers — a small town going about its life, unaware of the quiet mystery beginning to stir elsewhere, one that would soon draw the Sonnett family and Terry Miller into its unexpected orbit.

A Careful Hand

Terry stood there a moment, letting the librarian's words settle. *A map. An illustration.* The idea felt too big to hold all at once.

"Mrs. Norton," he said quietly, "if this really is a map… how would a person go about proving it? Or finding out what it's worth?"

She looked up at him over her glasses, her expression softening into something thoughtful and measured.

"Well," she said, "that depends on what you want to know. Age, origin, value — those are different questions. But you're not the only one with an old paper on your hands." She opened the drawer again and tapped the edge of the Civil War–era letter she'd shown him earlier. "I've written to the University of Virginia about this. Their special collections department has experts who can date handwriting, paper, ink. They're very good."

Terry felt a small spark of hope. "And you think they could help with mine too?"

"I expect so," she said. "When I hear back from them, I'll let you know. And if they're willing to look at my letter, they may be willing to look at your drawing as well."

He nodded, grateful. "Thank you, Mrs. Norton. I appreciate it."

"Just keep it safe," she said gently. "Old things like that don't come around often."

Terry patted the drawing in his shirt pocket as he stepped out onto the porch. The spring air met him with a bright, almost expectant warmth. He touched the pocket again, feeling the faint crackle of the paper beneath his fingers — a gesture that had already become a nervous habit.

"My ticket to…"

He didn't finish the sentence aloud.

But the words rose in him anyway, unbidden and shining.

…being more than ordinary.

He let the thought settle — surprising, a little frightening, but true — then started down the steps, the drawing close to his heart, unaware of how quickly that hope would be tested.

He climbed into his pickup and set his hat on the passenger seat. His hand drifted once more to the folded drawing in his pocket, as if to reassure himself it was still there. The engine rumbled to life with its familiar uneven idle, and he pulled away from the curb, Mrs. Norton's words about making a copy echoing in his mind as he drove down Chester Street.

A careful hand. Jake Sonnett.

By the time he reached the intersection where Chester fed into Royal Avenue, he eased the truck into the Safeway lot. He hadn't planned to stop, but habit and hunger nudged him through the doors.

Inside, the store smelled faintly of waxed floors and fresh produce. Bill Olinger, the manager, was straightening a display of canned peaches.

"Morning, Terry," he said. "Need anything special today?"

"Looking for a good cut of round steak," Terry replied. "I saw your ad in the Warren Sentinel this week."

Olinger nodded and disappeared into the back, returning with a wrapped package. "Just trimmed this myself. Last one. I'll be ordering more first of the week."

Terry paid, thanked him, and stepped back out into the sunlight. Before he even reached the truck, his hand went to his shirt pocket.

Still there.

He let out a breath he hadn't realized he was holding. "Good grief," he muttered. "I'm getting paranoid." But the truth was, the thought of losing that drawing made his stomach tighten. He promised himself — firmly — that he'd have Jake Sonnett make a copy. Soon.

He climbed into the truck and turned onto Royal Avenue, the package of meat on the seat beside him. By the time he reached his street, Terry had made up his mind.

He pulled into his driveway, the gravel crackling under the tires like dry corn husks. He cut the engine, sat for a breath, then went inside. The house felt still, as if holding its own kind of expectation.

After placing the steak in the refrigerator, he found the Sonnetts' number in the directory and tried to dial, but his finger slipped in the rotating dial.

"Dang this new dial phone," he muttered, hanging up and trying again. He much preferred the old system, when he picked up the receiver and a friendly operator would ask, "Number, please."

The phone rang twice before a young voice answered. "Sonnett residence — Jake speaking."

Terry smiled at the sound.

"Well, Jake, this is Terry Miller. I already saw you twice today and now I'm talking to you on the phone. I guess it's my lucky day. May I speak to your mother or father?"

"Mom's still out shopping with Emmett. And Dad's helping Grampa."

"Well, that's all right," Terry said. "Maybe you can pass along a message for me."

"Yes, sir. I can do that."

Terry hesitated — not out of uncertainty, but out of the natural care of a man who knew where the social boundaries lay and respected them.

"I understand you're quite the artist. Well, I need some artwork done," he said. "Copying an old picture I found this morning at the rummage sale. I was talking with Mrs. Norton at the library, and she recommended you."

Jake was surprised and pleased all at once. "Me?"

"Yes, sir," Terry said gently. "I'm sure you could do a good job. And I'll pay you for doing it. But listen — I need to talk to your parents first to make sure it's okay with them. I don't want to interfere with your schoolwork or the chores you've got at home. This is just an idea for now. Okay?"

Jake swallowed, trying to keep his voice steady. "I'll tell them, Mr. Miller. I promise."

"Good boy," Terry said, warmth in his voice. "And don't you worry — I'll explain everything to them. You just let your mom and dad know I called, and I'd appreciate a call back."

"I will, sir."

"All right then. You have yourself a good afternoon."

"You too, Mr. Miller."

Jake hung up the phone slowly, the receiver settling into its cradle with a soft click. For a moment he stood there, feeling taller somehow — as if the world had just nudged him a little closer to the person he hoped to become.

He remembered the art book and the Hardy Boys mystery waiting on the kitchen table. He also remembered that the Sky King show was on TV.

The Mistake

For the first time all day, Terry felt a lift in his chest — a small, bright sense that things were lining up. Jake sounded eager. Mrs. Norton had recommended him. Maybe, just maybe, this was going to turn into something.

He reached for the drawing—

—and his fingers slid straight through the side of his shirt pocket.

He froze.

The fabric gaped open under his touch, the stitching along the pocket seam torn wide. A loose thread swayed with his breath. He pushed his hand in again, hoping he'd somehow missed it.

Nothing.

A cold prickle climbed the back of his neck.

He checked the other pocket, then the first one again, pressing harder this time as if pressure alone might conjure the paper back into existence. But the pocket was empty.

This old shirt, he thought bitterly. I should've thrown it away.

He'd noticed the stitching fraying that morning. He'd ignored it. He regretted wearing it now — regretted it with a sharp, rising anger at himself. Careless. Stupid. He should've known better.

He hurried outside to the pickup, searching the seat, the floorboards, the narrow crack between the seat and the door. He even checked under the pedals, then the bed of the truck, though he knew the windows had been shut the whole way home.

Nothing.

The drawing — the brittle, irreplaceable drawing with the initials C.N. and A.M. — was gone.

He stood beside the truck for a long moment, the early afternoon sun illuminating everything. The hope he'd felt only minutes earlier drained out of him, leaving a hollow ache in its place.

I should've changed shirts. I should've been more careful. I should've known better.

He climbed into the truck and turned the key. The engine coughed, then settled into its familiar uneven rumble. He backed out of the driveway and headed the same way he'd come, eyes scanning the road, the gutters, the ditches.

"Think, Terry," he muttered. "Think."

But beneath the words was something deeper — a bruised truth rising in him again:

I finally had a chance to be more than plain Ol' Terry… and I let it fall right out of my pocket.

Of course this would happen.

He replayed the drive in his mind. Chester Street. The grocery store. Left on Royal Avenue. Then—

He snapped his fingers.

East Sixth Street and Happy Creek Road.

Now he remembered. He had slowed down just as he made the turn. Rolled down the window. Leaned halfway out to shout hello to his good buddy, Ray Shelley, who was on his front porch working with a power saw. They were both foremen at the Viscose plant.

Terry recalled laughing at something Ray hollered back about the Green Hornet — the nickname for a much-loved but tough-as-nails boss at the plant. He remembered leaning out of the truck window and how refreshing the breeze had felt.

I bet that's what tore the pocket.

He turned onto Happy Creek Road, driving slowly now, scanning the roadside. The late afternoon sun slanted across the pavement, catching bits of mica in the gravel and making them sparkle like tiny mirrors.

Nothing. He drove another twenty yards. Still nothing.

Terry pulled over near Ray Shelley's house and stepped out of the pickup, walking the shoulder of the road with his head bent, eyes scanning every scrap of paper, every leaf, every patch of grass. The wind had picked up, tossing little spirals of dust across the pavement.

Ray looked up from his porch rail, where he'd been resting after sweeping sawdust off the boards. "Terry? You lose something?"

Terry stopped, rubbed the back of his neck, and let out a long breath. "Yeah, Ray. I think I did. And I'm afraid it's something important."

Ray came down the steps, wiping his hands on his jeans. "Well now, tell me what you're looking for. Maybe I can help."

Terry hesitated, then reached into his shirt pocket — or what was left of it. The entire side seam had ripped open, the fabric gaping uselessly. He tapped the torn edge with two fingers, shame and frustration tightening his throat. "It was a drawing. Old. Fragile as dry leaves. Found it this morning in one of the Marigold boxes at the rummage sale."

Ray raised an eyebrow. "Marigold? That old place up on the ridge?"

"That's the one."

"What kind of drawing?"

Terry let out a breath that trembled just a little. "Hard to explain. Looked kind of like a sampler design. Vines and loops and two sets of initials — C.N. and A.M. It… it caught my eye, Ray. I don't know why. It just did. Felt like it didn't belong in a box with old picture frames and broken clocks."

Ray nodded, but his expression stayed practical. "Well, folks toss all kinds of things in those boxes. Most of it's not worth much."

Terry looked down the road, jaw tightening. "I was driving home, thinking about it. And when I turned onto your street, I leaned out the window to holler at you. Remember?"

Ray chuckled. "I remember you nearly fell out of the truck, carrying on about the Green Hornet."

"Yeah," Terry said, grimacing. "Well, I reckon that's when it happened. The pocket must have torn when I leaned out the window, and the wind caught the paper and pulled it right out. I didn't even feel it go."

Ray's face softened, but only a little. "Sorry to hear it. But if it was just a scrap of paper, maybe it's no great loss."

Terry swallowed. "It didn't feel like just a scrap. I was thinking it might be worth something."

Ray studied him, puzzled. "You really think it was something special?"

"I don't know," Terry said quietly. "I just… when I found it, I felt like I'd stumbled onto something special. Something that mattered to somebody once. And now it's gone, and I'm the fool who lost it."

Ray shook his head. "You're not a fool. But Terry, old paper is old paper. Could be worth something, could be worth nothing. No sense tearing yourself up over it."

Terry looked away, blinking against the sun. "Will you keep an eye out? If you see anything — anything at all — let me know."

"Sure thing, buddy," Ray said. "I'll check the yard, the ditch, even the neighbor's hedges. If it's around here, we'll spot it. But don't go thinking it's the end of the world."

Terry nodded, though the ache in his chest didn't ease. "Thanks, Ray."

"Anytime," Ray said, already scanning the grass with a practical, unhurried eye. "We'll find your paper if it's meant to be found."

But as Terry walked back to his truck, scanning the roadside once more, he couldn't shake the feeling that the drawing was already far from Happy Creek Road — carried off by wind, or by fate, or by someone who didn't understand what they held.

And somewhere down East Main, a boy on a bicycle was already pedaling hard, the drawing tucked neatly inside his shirt like a secret.

Old Means Money

The scrawny sixteen-year-old pedaled hard along East Main, his elbows jutting out like loose hinges, the folded drawing tucked inside his shirt. The late-afternoon sun flashed off the shop windows as he zipped past, turning the glass fronts into brief, blinding mirrors. But Eddie Combs kept his eyes fixed on his destination — the squat brick storefront of Harlan's Pawn & Jewelry Shop, sandwiched between the Duck Inn and Frank's Barber Shop — a place where fortunes were small but possible, and where a boy with quick hands and quicker hopes might turn a scrap of nothing into a dollar or two.

Not an hour earlier he'd been rummaging through the ditch along Sixth Street, hunting unsuccessfully for returnable "pop" bottles. He was always on the lookout for anything he could turn into a little cash. Folks said he had a nose for opportunity — and a talent for trouble.

He was halfway along the ditch when something pale caught his eye — a scrap of paper flapping in the breeze, snagged against a tuft of grass.

"What've we got here?" he muttered, crouching down.

He lifted the folded sheet with a kind of rough care — not respect, exactly, but the wary touch of someone who knows old things sometimes mean old value. Coins. Stamps. Documents. Anything a man behind a counter might pay for.

He unfolded it.

"Huh," he said softly. "Looks old."

Old means money. Or at least the chance of it.

He folded it again — not gently — and slipped it inside his shirt, close to the skin where sweat and dust had already begun to gather.

"Maybe old Wally'll know what it is," he said aloud, already picturing the man's eyebrows climbing behind those thick glasses.

He didn't notice the tiny corner that flaked off in his hand. He didn't notice the faint tear along one edge.

And he didn't notice Terry Miller's pickup truck turning onto the street behind him, moving slowly, the driver's eyes scanning the roadside with growing worry.

By the time Terry passed, Eddie was already pedaling hard toward the pawn shop, the drawing thumping lightly against his ribs.

He skidded to a stop in front of the shop, dropped his bike against the wall, and pushed open the door. A bell overhead gave a tired jingle.

Inside, the place smelled of old metal and older stories, with a faint overlay of Air Wick trying its best to civilize the air.

Wally Harlan looked up from behind the counter, his thick glasses magnifying his eyes until they seemed too large for his face. He was about fifty, a little overweight, his shirt sleeves rolled past his elbows and held up by a pair of tired suspenders. A chewed-down cigar stub clung to the corner of his mouth, unlit but clearly a permanent fixture. With his heavy jaw and thinning hair, he had that Ernest-Borgnine look—part genial, part dangerous, depending on how the light hit him.

Years ago he'd been a boxer, and though the belly had come in and the breath had shortened, the hands were still quick—strong, fast hands that could appraise a watch, palm a coin, or snatch something fragile out of a kid's grip before it hit the floor.

Around town, people spoke of him in lowered voices, the way folks do when they're not sure whether a story is true or just old smoke drifting from an older fire. Unsavory-looking out-of-towners were often seen coming and going from his shop—men who didn't look like they were here for antiques or musical instruments—and that only fed the quiet suspicion that Wally had, or once had, connections better left unmentioned. Nothing proven, nothing recent, just the kind of whispers that cling to a man who never seems surprised by anything brought across his counter.

"Eddie Combs," he said, suspicion settling into his voice. "What've you got this time?"

Eddie grinned, all bravado and hope. "Something old. Maybe valuable."

Harlan snorted. "Everything you bring me is 'maybe valuable.' Let's see it."

Eddie laid the folded paper on the counter. Harlan reached for it with surprising gentleness, unfolding it slowly. His expression changed almost at once — not excitement, but something quieter, deeper. Recognition, maybe. Or memory.

"Well now," he murmured. "Where'd you get this?"

"Found it," Eddie said. "In the ditch on Sixth Street just past the grocery store."

Harlan didn't look up. His eyes traced the initials — C.N. and A.M. — the delicate vines, the faint border. He touched the edge and another tiny flake broke off, drifting like a dry leaf.

"This is old," he said quietly. "Older than you know."

"So… is it worth anything?" Eddie asked, leaning forward.

Harlan folded the drawing again, more carefully than Eddie ever had. "Maybe. Maybe not. But I'll tell you this — it's not something you should've been carrying around inside your shirt, all sweaty and dirty."

Eddie's face fell. "So you don't want it?"

Harlan hesitated — just long enough for Eddie to feel the hope slipping.

"I didn't say that."

He opened the cash drawer and pulled out a few bills. "I'll give you five dollars for it."

Eddie's eyes widened. Five dollars was a fortune in his world.

"Deal," he said quickly.

Harlan handed over the money, then slipped the drawing into a manila envelope and wrote something on the front — a name Eddie didn't catch.

As Eddie left the shop, the bell jingling behind him, Harlan stood very still, staring at the envelope in his hands. The shop around him seemed to fade, the dust motes hanging in the air like suspended thoughts.

He reached for his Rolodex, thumbed through the cards, and dialed a number.

"Hello. Is this Whitmore? Yeah? Well, Professor… I think I found that document you're looking for. I know it's late, but I'll stay open, if you can come see it."

***

Jake had barely set the receiver back in its cradle when he heard the family car pull into the driveway and give a quick honk — the horn gave that little toot his mother used when she wanted him to come out and help her carry something into the house.

He stepped out onto the porch just as she opened the car door. "I believe you left your drawing pad on the back seat," she said. "Take it inside, will you?"

He ran out, picked up the pad, thinking of all the sketches waiting to be born on its empty pages. He headed back into the house.

"Emmett, stop swinging that bag around before you break something," Mrs. Sonnett said, her tone carrying the weary patience of a woman who had spent the last hour chasing a ten -year-old through four stores.

"I'm not swinging it," Emmett insisted, swinging it.

Jake hurried into the front hall, unable to keep the excitement from his face.

"Boy, am I glad you're home!" he said, almost tripping over the rug in his eagerness.

His mother looked up, surprised by the greeting. "Well, hello to you too. Did you get your books?"

"Yes, ma'am," Jake said, but the words tumbled out too fast, as if they were only the warm-up act for what he really wanted to say. "And Mr. Miller called."

That stopped her. She set her purse on the hall table. "Terry Miller? What did he want?"

Jake drew a breath, trying to sound calm and grown-up, but the glow in his eyes gave him away. "He said he needs some artwork done. Copying an old picture he found at the rummage sale. He was talking with Mrs. Norton, and she recommended me."

"You?" Emmett said, dropping his bag entirely. "Why you?"

"Because I can draw," Jake said, with a dignity that made his mother's mouth soften.

Mrs. Sonnett brushed a strand of hair from her forehead, studying her older son. "What exactly did he say?"

"He said he's sure I could do a good job, and he'd pay me. But he wants to talk to you and Dad first. He said he doesn't want to interfere with my schoolwork or chores."

That last part — the respect in it — seemed to settle something in her. She nodded slowly.

"Well," she said, "that sounds like Terry. Always careful. Always polite."

Jake couldn't hold back his smile any longer. "Mom… he wants me to copy an old drawing. Me."

"I heard you the first time," she said, but there was warmth in her voice now, a quiet pride she didn't try to hide. "We'll talk to your father when he gets home. If Mr. Miller thinks you're the right one for the job, we'll hear him out."

Jake felt the words land inside him like a small, steady flame.

Emmett tugged at his sleeve. "Does this mean you're gonna be famous?"

Jake rolled his eyes. "No, dummy."

But he was still smiling.

Mrs. Sonnett picked up her purse again. "All right, boys. Help me put these things away. And Jake — you can tell your father the whole story when he gets home."

"Yes, ma'am," he said, already imagining how he'd say it, how his father might nod in that quiet way of his.

As they moved toward the kitchen, the house felt different somehow — as if a new thread had been woven into the day, fine and bright, pulling gently toward something none of them could yet see.

Rare Means Money

Professor Daniel Whitmore arrived on East Main just as the sun was lowering behind the ridge, throwing long shadows across the storefronts. He paused outside Harlan's Pawn & Jewelry, taking in the dusty window display — a jumble of pocket watches, tarnished silver, and a mandolin with one string missing. It was not the sort of place he imagined history would hide itself, but then again, history had a habit of choosing unlikely corners.

He pushed open the door. The bell overhead gave a thin, metallic jingle.

Wally Harlan looked up from behind the counter. His thick glasses caught the light, turning his eyes into two pale moons.

"You Whitmore?" he asked.

"I am," the professor said, stepping forward. "Thanks for staying open late."

Harlan nodded, slow and deliberate, as though he were measuring the professor's worth by the way he crossed the room. He reached under the counter and brought out a manila envelope — the same one Eddie Combs had watched him label.

He laid it on the counter but did not open it.

Whitmore's breath tightened. He recognized the weight of the moment — the possibility that something long lost might be resting inches from his hand.

"You said you found a document," Whitmore said, trying to keep his voice even.

"I said I *might've* found something," Harlan corrected. "Depends what you're lookin' for."

Whitmore bristled inwardly. He disliked men who played coy with facts. "I'm cataloging the Marigold papers. Some items were separated from the estate before donation. I've been trying to locate them."

Harlan tapped the envelope with one thick finger. "Well, this here wasn't in no estate box. A boy brought it in. Found it on the side of the road. Someone probably threw it out of their car. Litterbugs."

Whitmore's jaw tightened. "May I see it?"

Harlan hesitated just long enough to make a point, then slid the envelope toward him.

Whitmore opened it carefully. When he unfolded the drawing, the room seemed to tilt. The delicate vines, the looping lines, the initials C.N. and A.M. — none of it appeared in the Marigold ledger. No mention. No description. Nothing.

And yet here it was. A piece of the story he hadn't even known was missing.

"My word," he whispered.

Harlan watched him closely. "Mean something to you?"

Whitmore tried to control his reaction, but the excitement leaked through — a quickening of breath, a softening of the eyes. "It's… unexpected."

"Unexpected good," Harlan said, "or unexpected expensive?"

Whitmore stiffened. "I'll need to authenticate it."

Harlan's eyebrows rose. "Authenticate? Looks old to me."

"Age alone isn't proof," Whitmore said. "I'll need to bring in a specialist."

Harlan leaned back, crossing his arms. "Specialist, huh. Sounds like you're fixin' to take it outta here."

"I would, of course, return it," Whitmore said, though the words felt thin even to him. "But I can't make an offer until I'm certain of its provenance."

Harlan snorted. "Provenance. Fancy word for 'you want it.'"

Whitmore flushed. "I want it properly documented."

"And I want five hundred dollars," Harlan said flatly.

Whitmore stared at him. "Five hundred? That's absurd."

"Not to me."

"It's not even listed in the Marigold inventory," Whitmore said. "There's no record of it."

"Then maybe it's rare," Harlan said, shrugging. "Rare things cost money."

Whitmore felt the heat rising in his face. He considered Harlan a crude man — a man who saw history only as something to be priced, not understood. And Harlan, for his part, saw in Whitmore the kind of educated fellow who thought he could talk a man down with long words and thin smiles.

They stood there, two men separated by temperament, education, and the fragile sheet of paper between them.

"I won't pay five hundred," Whitmore said.

"And I won't let it walk out that door for less," Harlan replied.

Whitmore folded the drawing with care and slid it back into the envelope. "Then we're at an impasse."

"Looks that way."

Whitmore hesitated, the weight of disappointment settling on him like dust. "If you change your mind…"

"I won't," Harlan said.

Whitmore nodded once, curtly, and turned toward the door. The bell jingled as he stepped out into the fading light.

Behind him, Harlan watched through the window, the envelope still resting on the counter.

An Odd Story

Terry had just come in from checking the truck bed for the third time — as if the drawing might somehow have blown *into* it instead of out — when the telephone rang. The sound startled him; he was wound tight as a fence wire.

He lifted the receiver. "Hello."

"Terry? It's Ray."

Terry felt a flicker of hope. "Ray — you find something?"

"Well… maybe. Maybe not. But I've got an odd story for you."

Terry sat down at the kitchen table, bracing himself. "Go on."

Ray cleared his throat, the way he did when he wasn't sure how to begin. "My wife just got home from takin' Ray Jr. to Frank's Barber Shop. You know — the one next door to Harlan's pawn place."

"I know it," Terry said, his pulse quickening.

"Well," Ray continued, "she was coming out of the barber shop, holding Ray Jr.'s hand, when that Combs boy — Eddie — near ran 'em both over with his bicycle. She said he came flying down the sidewalk like a bat outta hell."

Terry closed his eyes. "Eddie Combs."

"Yeah. She said she gave him a piece of her mind, too. But he didn't even slow down. Just barreled right past her and straight into Harlan's shop."

Terry's breath caught. "Into the pawn shop?"

"That's right. And she said she could see clear as day through that big plate-glass window. Eddie rushes in, all worked up, and hands Harlan a piece of paper. Looked old. Looked… delicate."

Terry felt the room tilt. "A drawing?"

"That's what she said. Some kind of antique looking thing like a map or something. Harlan gives him money — she couldn't see how much — and Eddie bolts right back out the door. She hollered after him again, but he was already halfway down the block."

Terry pressed a hand to his forehead. "Lord, help me."

Ray's voice softened. "Terry… you think that was the old paper you lost?"

"I don't think," Terry said quietly. "I know."

There was a long pause on the line — the kind of silence that only exists between old friends, where worry and sympathy can sit side by side without either man needing to name them.

Ray finally spoke. "What're you gonna do?"

Terry looked toward the window, where the late-day sun was slipping behind the ridge. "I don't know yet. But if Eddie sold it to Harlan… then Harlan's got it now."

Ray exhaled slowly. "That ain't good."

"No," Terry said. "It ain't."

Another pause.

"Terry," Ray said gently, "I'll keep lookin' around here, just in case. But sounds like that drawing's already changed hands."

Terry nodded, though Ray couldn't see it. "Thanks, Ray. I appreciate you calling."

"You'd do the same for me."

"I would," Terry said. "And Ray… tell your wife I'm sorry she and Ray Jr. got scared."

"I will. You take care now."

Terry hung up the receiver and sat for only a moment, the decision forming as quickly as the fear. There was only one thing to do. He knew it was late but if he hurried maybe he could get there just in time before Harlan closed up shop for the day.

He grabbed his jacket from the hook, shrugged it on, and was out the door before the screen had time to settle behind him. He climbed into his truck, turned the key hard, and headed straight for Main Street.

The shop looked empty, but the neon OPEN sign in the window was still glowing as Terry pulled up to the curb. He checked the dashboard clock — later than he thought. The pawn shop usually closed early on Saturdays.

The sign flicked off.

"Shoot," Terry muttered, already out of the truck.

He ran across the sidewalk just as Wally Harlan reached for the door, key in hand. The lock clicked, and Harlan began to pull the door shut.

"Hold up," Terry said, catching the edge of the door with his palm before it closed. "Just need a minute."

Harlan frowned, clearly irritated, but he stepped back and let Terry slip inside. The bell overhead gave its thin, metallic jingle — a sound that seemed to disapprove of the intrusion.

Wally Harlan looked at Terry, his thick glasses catching the light. "You know it's past closing time," he said, irritation edging every word. "What can I do for you?"

Terry forced a polite smile. "Just lookin' around. I collect old things sometimes. For the right price."

Harlan's eyes narrowed. "You forced your way in here just to look around?" His tone carried his annoyance — the kind of irritation that comes from a man who'd already decided his day was over and didn't appreciate it being reopened.

Terry kept his voice even. "Won't take but a minute."

Harlan grunted, unimpressed. "Anything in particular?"

Terry let his eyes wander over the shelves — pocket watches, chipped china, a stack of old postcards — before settling on the counter. "Heard a boy came in earlier. Eddie Combs. Brought you a drawing."

Harlan's expression didn't change, but something in his posture did — a slight stiffening, like a bird dog alerting to the sound of its prey.

"Boy brings in all kinds of junk," Harlan said.

"This wasn't junk," Terry replied quietly. "It was mine."

Harlan's eyebrows rose. "Yours, huh?"

"Eddie found it on the road," Terry said. "Blew out of my truck. I'd like it back. I'll pay you double whatever you gave him."

Harlan leaned back, crossing his arms. "That so?"

"It is."

A long silence stretched between them, thick as humidity in July.

Finally Harlan said, "Well, that's a shame."

"What is?"

"I already got a buyer interested."

Terry felt his stomach drop. "Who?"

"Man knows his history," Harlan said. "Name's Whitmore."

Terry swallowed hard. "So you're sayin' you won't sell it back to me."

"I'm sayin' it's worth more than double what I paid that boy," Harlan replied. "And I don't do charity."

Terry's jaw tightened. "It's not charity. It's right."

Harlan shrugged. "Right don't keep the lights on."

Terry stared at him, the anger rising slow and steady — not hot, but deep, the kind that comes from knowing you're being played by a man who enjoys the game.

"Mr. Harlan," he said quietly, "that drawing wasn't meant to be in a ditch. And it sure wasn't meant to be sold off to the highest bidder."

Harlan tapped the counter with one thick finger. "World don't work on 'meant to,' Mr. Miller. It works on who's holdin' the goods."

Terry took a breath, steadying himself. "Then I'll find another way."

"You do that," Harlan said, already turning away.

Terry walked out of the shop, the bell jingling behind him like a small, mocking laugh. He stood on the sidewalk for a long moment, staring at the fading light on East Main.

He had lost the drawing once by accident. He would not lose it again by giving up.

Somewhere behind him, in that dim little shop, the past was sitting in a manila envelope — silently waiting for someone to claim it.

And Terry Miller intended to be that someone.

The Second Chance

Jake was still glowing from the offer from Terry Miller to do a drawing for him, pacing the kitchen with a grin he couldn't hide. His mother was slicing carrots at the counter, the smell of onions and butter filling the room. Emmett sat on the floor, making his model airplane swoop under the table, complete with sound effects that grew louder every time he forgot he wasn't outside.

The back door opened, and Bill Sonnett stepped inside, brushing dust from his sleeves. He filled a doorway the way certain men do — not because of their size, but because of presence. Years of selling Chevrolets at Parkway had given him an easy confidence, a way of talking that made people feel they'd known him longer than they had. The Scoutmaster in him added a layer of calm authority, and the Jaycees added just enough mischief to keep him from seeming too perfect.

"Evening," he said, hanging his cap on the hook. "Whew. Dad had me in that garage all morning. Found things I hadn't seen since I was a boy." He gave a tired smile. "And just before the post office closed, Mother remembered she needed stamps. So I ran down there."

Mrs. Sonnett glanced over. "Did you get them?"

"Sure did." Bill washed his hands at the sink. "Phil was working the window. Told me Terry Miller showed him some kind of old drawing. Said it looked valuable. You know how he likes to report the latest news."

Jake's heart jumped. "Mr. Miller called here," he said, trying to sound calm. "He… he wants me to copy a drawing for him."

Bill's eyebrows lifted, but with quiet recognition rather than surprise. "Well now, Jake. That's something."

He said it gently, but there was weight behind it — the kind of weight that comes from a man who has learned not to take his children's gifts for granted.

Bill and Jeanie had lost their first child, little Billy Jr., before he'd even learned to walk. The grief had nearly hollowed them out. Ever since, they'd treated Jake and Emmett like blessings they'd been given a second chance to protect. Encouragement came easily to them; worry came even easier.

"Besides talking to Mr. Miller on the phone, what else did you do today?"

Jake nodded, suddenly shy. "I got a big drawing pad at the rummage sale. It's great. And I went to the library and checked out a couple of books — one, a new Hardy Boys mystery, one a big art book. I was going to practice drawing after supper."

Bill smiled — a small, proud smile that warmed the room. "Sounds like you've had a full day."

He dried his hands and leaned back against the counter, watching his family with that quiet, settled contentment that came from knowing exactly where he belonged. "Well now," he said, "sounds like everybody's been busy today except me. I just crawled around in Dad's garage for four hours and came out looking like I'd been wrestling a coal stove."

Jeanie snorted softly. "You *always* come out of that garage looking like that."

"That's because Dad never throws anything away," Bill said. "I found a box of spark plugs from 1938. And a roller skate missing both front wheels."

Emmett looked up from under the table. "Why would anybody keep roller skates with no wheels?"

Bill pointed a finger at him. "That, son, is a question your grandfather has never once answered in his entire life."

Jake laughed, the sound bubbling up from the excitement he'd been trying to contain. "Maybe he's saving them for parts."

"Parts for *what*?" Bill asked. "A man with no feet?"

Jeanie shook her head, trying not to smile. "Bill, honestly."

Bill winked at her. "Just keeping the mood light, honey. You slice onions like you're preparing for a funeral."

She swatted him with the back of her hand, but her eyes softened. Bill had always been able to make her laugh — even in the darkest days after they lost Billy Jr. Sometimes she wondered if that was how they'd survived the trauma.

Bill turned back to Jake. "So tell me about this drawing. Mr. Miller must think a lot of your work to ask you to copy something for him."

Jake's ears reddened. "I don't know if he thinks a lot of it. He said Mrs. Norton recommended me." He pronounced *recommended* with deliberate care.

Bill nodded slowly. "That's how it starts, you know. One person sees what you can do. Then another. Then another. Next thing you know, you're painting signs for half the county."

Jake grinned. "I don't want to paint signs."

"No," Bill said, "you want to paint *pictures.* And that's a perfectly fine thing."

Emmett swooped his airplane under Jake's legs. "I want to be a pilot!"

"You want to be a *lot* of things," Jeanie said. "Yesterday you wanted to be a cowboy."

"I can be both," Emmett insisted. "A cowboy pilot."

Bill chuckled. "Well, if anybody could rope a steer from an airplane, it'd be you."

Emmett beamed.

Bill reached for a carrot slice from the cutting board and popped it into his mouth. "You know," he said thoughtfully, "when I was Jake's age, I didn't have half his talent. I was too busy trying to impress girls by throwing rocks at fence posts."

Jeanie raised an eyebrow. "And how did that work out for you?"

"Well," Bill said, gesturing around the kitchen, "I eventually married the prettiest girl in town, so I guess it worked out fine."

Jeanie blushed, and Jake rolled his eyes in the way boys do when their parents get sentimental.

Bill grew quiet for a moment, his gaze drifting to his sons — one sprawled on the floor with a toy airplane, the other pacing with a dream in his hands. "You boys," he said softly, "you're our second chance. Your mama and I… we don't take that lightly."

Jeanie's knife slowed, her breath catching just a little. She didn't look up, but she didn't need to. Bill's words hung in the warm kitchen air like a blessing.

Jake swallowed, unsure what to say, but feeling the weight of his father's pride settle gently on his shoulders.

Bill clapped his hands once, breaking the moment before it grew too heavy. "All right! Who's hungry? I could eat a horse."

"You'll get meatloaf," Jeanie said, "and you'll be grateful."

"I'm always grateful," Bill said, kissing her cheek as he passed. "Especially when it's meatloaf."

Emmett zoomed his airplane through the air. "Can I have extra mashed potatoes?"

"You can have extra *if* you wash your hands," Jeanie said.

Emmett groaned. "Why does everything good start with washing your hands?"

"Because," Bill said, scooping him up, "clean hands make for clean living."

"And clean living," Jake added, grinning, "makes for clean plates."

Bill laughed. "Now *that's* my boy."

The kitchen filled with the sounds of drawers opening, plates clinking, and the soft hum of a family settling into the evening — unaware that the drawing Jake was supposed to copy, the one now in the possession of the local pawn shop owner, was already beginning to tug their lives toward something none of them could yet imagine.

The Delay

The Sonnett family gathered around the table, the light softening as the sun dipped behind the ridge. Bill bowed his head for grace, then passed the biscuits and waited while everyone helped themselves. After a few bites, he cleared his throat and glanced around the table. "All right," he said, lowering his fork. "You'll never guess what your granddad started talking about today while we were cleaning out his garage."

Jeanie, knowing her father-in-law all too well, gave Bill a cautious look — the kind that meant she could already tell this story was about to drift a shade off-color. "Bill…"

He waved a hand. "Now, now — it's nothing bad. Just one of his old stories. Out of the blue he starts talking about the Marigold estate."

Jake's head lifted a little at that.

Bill went on, "Says when he was a boy, he and his buddies used to hike up there because everybody said the place was haunted. And the old woman who lived there — Miss Alethea — well, folks claimed she talked to ghosts."

Emmett's eyes widened. "Did she really?"

Bill chuckled. "Depends on who you ask. The gossipy old ladies in town said all kinds of things about her. Called her a witch, said she was up to no good. And apparently Miss Alethea got wind of it."

Jeanie sighed. "Bill…"

"Oh, hush now," he said, grinning. "The boys are old enough. It's the 1960s. They hear worse on TV."

He leaned in a little, lowering his voice for effect. "So, Miss Alethea decides she's had enough of the gossip. Sends out invitations — formal invitations — to all those ladies for a little afternoon gathering at her house."

Jake and Emmett leaned forward at the same time.

"Now here's the part your mother doesn't want me to tell," Bill said, giving Jeanie a playful wink. "Miss Alethea had herself a still."

Jake blinked. "What's a still?"

Jeanie groaned. "Bill…"

Bill patted Jake's hand. "A still is a way folks used to make their own liquor. Moonshine. Applejack. Strong stuff. Not for kids, and not for most grown-ups either."

Jeanie muttered, "Wonderful. Just wonderful."

Bill continued, undeterred. "Anyway, Miss Alethea serves these ladies a 'special drink' — her finest applejack brandy — and they don't have the slightest idea what they're sipping. Now get this. They go home so drunk they can barely walk straight. Embarrassed themselves all over town. Can you imagine that?"

Emmett burst out laughing. Jake tried not to, but failed.

Bill spread his hands. "And after that? Not one of those ladies ever again said another bad word about Miss Alethea. Not a whisper. Their gossip died right then and there."

Jake laughed, the sound bright and unguarded. Even Jeanie couldn't help smiling as she shook her head. "Your father," she said, "is impossible."

Bill grinned. "Maybe. But it's a good story."

When dinner was over and the dishes were washed, and after Emmett had wandered off to his room, Bill put a hand on Jake's shoulder.

"Come on," he said. "Let's call Mr. Miller."

Jake didn't move at first. He was staring past the table, eyes unfocused, as if he were still sitting inside the story his father had told.

"Jake," Bill said again, a little more firmly.

Jake blinked, coming back to himself. "Yes, sir."

"Let's call Mr. Miller."

He followed his father to the hallway phone, heart beating so strongly he could feel it.

Bill dialed, spoke quietly, listened, nodded. Jake watched every flicker of his father's expression.

When Bill hung up, he turned to Jake with a steady, reassuring smile.

"Well," he said, "there's been a momentary delay."

Jake's breath caught. "Did he say how long?"

"No," Bill said gently. "But he sounded grateful you're willing to help. He just needs a little time to get things sorted."

Bill rubbed his big hand across Jake's hair. "Good things don't disappear just because they take a little longer."

Jake nodded, the knot in his chest easing. "Okay."

"You'll get your chance," Bill said. "I can feel it."

After hearing the disappointing news, Jake tried to act calm — tried to nod, as if the delay didn't matter.

He drifted to his room, the two library books stacked neatly on his desk, the drawing pad from the rummage sale propped beside them. He touched it lightly, imagining all the drawings that would fill it.

He trusted his father — and when his father said something, it had a way of turning out true.

Jake remembered last summer, the night before the county fair, when he'd wanted to throw away his charcoal drawing because the shading looked wrong. His father had told him to sleep on it. Jake had listened — he fixed the shading in the morning and won second place. He still kept the ribbon tacked to the side of his dresser mirror.

He took a breath, letting that memory steady him.

Glancing at the clock, he saw that the time was 8:12 p.m., and he had to be up before six. He was a paper boy, and he knew the Sunday edition of the paper was bigger, heavier, and took more time to deliver.

Paper routes didn't care about art or delays or antique drawings. They cared about boys who showed up on time.

His father's voice echoed gently in his mind: "Good things don't disappear just because they take a little longer."

Jake lay back on his bed, staring at the ceiling, letting the excitement settle into something warm and steady instead of jittery. He wasn't going to let a delay ruin this. He wasn't going to let doubt creep in.

He was a working kid — he knew how to wait, how to show up, how to keep going even when he was tired.

He smiled to himself in the dimming light. Mr. Miller would call back.

His father said so.

***

Saturday evening settled over Front Royal the way a quilt settles over a sleeping child — soft, familiar, and carrying the weight of a hundred ordinary stories. But inside a few scattered houses, the night was anything but restful.

Terry Miller lay awake in the dark, staring at the ceiling as though it might offer an answer. He'd always been a man who tried to do right, even when the world didn't make it easy. But tonight the drawing — that fragile scrap of someone else's past — pressed on him like a stone. He felt he'd failed it somehow, and the feeling wouldn't let him sleep.

Across town, Mrs. Norton washed her supper dishes with a quiet contentment. She believed she'd set something good in motion that day, and the thought warmed her like a small lamp in a dark room. She had no notion of the trouble brewing around that drawing, nor would she have believed it if someone told her.

Wally Harlan, over at the pawn shop, paced the narrow aisles long after closing. He kept turning the key to the back room in his hand, thinking about the drawing locked inside. He told himself he was only being cautious, but the truth was he was afraid — afraid of losing out, afraid of being caught, afraid of the man he was thinking of calling.

Eddie Combs, who had started all this without meaning to, sat on the edge of his bed thinking about what he might buy with his five dollars. He didn't bother with exact plans; he never did. Mostly he just felt good having the money at all. Still, every so often he glanced toward the hallway, hoping his father wouldn't come in and beat him and take it.

Eddie liked to look on the bright side, but tonight he was careful with it, holding his little bit of luck close.

And up on the second floor of the Hotel Royal, Professor Daniel Whitmore sat alone at the small writing desk in Room 214. The brass lamp cast a warm circle of light over his open notebook, but the page remained mostly blank. He had come to Front Royal to study the past, yet somehow the past had reached out and taken hold of him instead. The drawing — its vines, its initials, its quiet mystery — tugged at him with a persistence he couldn't explain. Outside his window, the neon HOTEL ROYAL sign flickered against the dusk, and he wondered, not for the first time, whether he had stumbled into something meant for him.

So the town settled into night — some sleeping easy, some not sleeping at all — each one holding a small piece of a story that was quietly gathering itself, like a river drawing its tributaries together before the bend.

The Lost Coin

Sunday morning came to Front Royal with a soft, forgiving light, the kind that makes a man believe the world might still have room for second chances. Terry Miller stepped out onto his porch, rubbing the sleep from his eyes, though he hadn't had much of it.

He'd woken more than once during the night, bothered by troubling dreams he couldn't quite hold onto — he remembered he was out on the river in a small boat, trying to paddle against a current that wouldn't let him move. No matter how hard he dug in, the boat just sat there, rocking in place as if held by an anchor while the water slid past on either side. By morning the details had slipped away, leaving only the uneasy feeling of frustration and effort without progress, the kind that clings to a man long after the dream itself has faded away.

Across town, in a cramped apartment that smelled of old coffee and stale cigarettes, Wally Harlan paced the worn linoleum like a man walking the length of his own worry. The drawing — that fragile, dangerous thing — lay on the table where he'd set it down, and the longer he looked at it, the more trouble he imagined it could bring. *What if Miller accuses me of selling stolen goods? What if he contacts the authorities and they start asking questions? What if they want to look at my records?* He wiped his palms on his pants, picked up the phone, and dialed a number he knew he shouldn't.

"Yeah… it's me," he said, voice low. "Listen, Pike, I've got something valuable. A really old document. Worth a lot. No, I can't say more over the line."

There was a long pause.

"Tomorrow morning. Your place. First thing."

He hung up. Wally Harlan sat in silence hoping that this would solve his problem.

In the meantime, Jake Sonnett delivered his newspapers and hurried home. His family was planning to picnic at Dickey Ridge that afternoon.

After a sleepless night, Terry Miller decided to drive across town to the newsstand on Main Street, the air cool and clean, and bought himself a copy of *The Washington Post*. He didn't know exactly what he was looking for in those pages — maybe distraction, maybe reassurance — but the rustle of the paper in his hands felt steadying somehow.

Instead of returning home immediately, he did something he hadn't planned on. He turned toward the Methodist church.

He wasn't what you'd call a regular, but he knew when a man needed a little lift, and this morning he surely did. As he reached the steps, he heard Miss Rudacille playing the organ inside and the rhythmic tramp of boots behind him. The Randolph-Macon Academy cadets — the "Jakes," as the town called them — were marching in formation, crisp and straight-backed, filing into the sanctuary with the solemnity of young men practicing adulthood.

Terry slipped into a pew near the back. The stained-glass windows glowed with the rising sun, and the familiar creak of the wooden pews felt like an old friend settling in beside him.

When it was time for the sermon, Reverend Johnson opened his Bible to the parable of the lost coin. He told it plain and simple — the way country preachers do — about a woman who had ten silver coins and lost one. She didn't shrug it off or tell herself she could get by with nine. No, she lit a lamp, swept her whole house, and searched every corner until she found it. And when she did, she called her neighbors to rejoice with her.

"Sometimes in life," he said, "we lose things that matter — not just coins, but hope, direction, courage, even a sense of who we are. And when that happens, God doesn't give up on us. He lights a lamp. He sweeps the corners of our lives. He searches until the lost thing is found again. What is lost is never forgotten. And what is misplaced is never abandoned."

Terry felt those words settle into him like warm water easing a knot. He didn't know whether the preacher meant the drawing, or his own sense of purpose, or something deeper still. But for the first time in days, he felt the faint stirrings of hope. He wouldn't give up.

After the benediction, he stepped back into the sunlight feeling a little lighter. He decided the afternoon would be his own. No worrying, no pacing, no turning things over until they lost their shape.

He went home, set the radio to the Washington Senators game — "First in war, first in peace, and last in the American League," as the old joke went — and let the familiar crackle of the broadcast fill the room.

He cooked himself a steak, simple and satisfying, and ate it with the windows open to the spring air.

By sundown, the ache of the past two days had settled into something he could carry. He washed his plate, turned off the radio, and headed to bed early. Monday would come soon enough, and with it the work he knew how to do.

For now, he let the quiet take him.

And so Sunday passed — quietly, gently — each person carrying their own hopes and worries, unaware of how closely their paths were beginning to run.

The day ended the way days often do in Front Royal: with porch lights glowing, the river whispering in the distance, and a sense that something just beyond understanding was gathering itself for the days ahead.

The Argument

Early Monday morning Wally Harlan drove down Royal Avenue with his jaw clenched and his fingers drumming the steering wheel. The morning was gray and close, the kind that made a man feel the week pressing down on him before it even began. He pulled into the narrow space behind the old apartment building next to Nick's Good Food Diner.

The building was a tired brick relic with peeling paint and windows that hadn't been washed since Truman was president. Harlan killed the engine, wiped his palms on his pants, grabbed the manila envelope, entered the building, and climbed the stairs to the second floor, each step creaking under his weight.

He knocked.

The door opened a crack, and Lenny Pike's sharp eyes appeared — eyes that missed nothing and forgave even less. He swung the door wide without a word.

Inside, the apartment was dim and stale. A single lamp burned on a cluttered table crowded with newspapers, ashtrays, and the remains of last night's supper. The air smelled of old smoke and fried onions.

"You bring it?" Pike asked.

Harlan nodded and reached into his coat, pulling out the envelope. He held it carefully, almost reverently. "Right here."

Pike didn't take it. He just watched Harlan, the way a man watches a dog he isn't sure won't bite.

"So," Pike said, "leave it with me and I'll contact you when I sell it. Then we can settle up."

"I want to close the deal," Harlan said. "Right now. I want to be paid. You said you had a buyer."

"I said I *might* have a buyer," Pike corrected. "And I don't pay a dime until I know what I'm holding."

Harlan's face reddened. "We talked about this last night."

"We talked," Pike said, shrugging. "Talking's cheap."

Harlan's breath came faster. "You're not pulling a fast one on me, Pike. Not this time."

Their voices were getting louder.

Pike's smile was thin and humorless. "A fast one? Listen, you brought me a piece of paper from a rummage sale. I'm doing you a favor even looking at it. Watches and jewelry are a sure thing, but I'm taking a chance on a scrap of paper."

"It's worth plenty – at least two-hundred," Harlan snapped. "I know it is. And you know it too, or you wouldn't have told me to come here at the crack of dawn."

Pike stepped closer, his voice dropping. "You don't tell me what something's worth. That's my job. You want money? You wait until I say so. I have contacts."

"Your contacts — ha! Your contacts are just other pawn shops, you scum!"

Harlan's hands tightened into fists. "I'm not leaving without getting paid." He shoved Pike.

Pike's eyes hardened. "Listen to me. You'll get paid when I get paid. Take it or leave it!"

He shook his fist.

"It's an antique drawing, for God's sake. Worth more than the other crap you sell."

Something in Harlan broke then — fear, pride, desperation all tangled together. "You always do this," he said, voice shaking. "You string people along. You take what you want and leave the rest of us holding nothing. I have a mind to let the police know about the Bruno incident."

Pike's hand moved — quick, practiced, almost casual.

Harlan froze. Pike's gun glinted in the dim light.

"You're not going to snitch on me," Pike shouted.

Royal Avenue – Two Minutes Earlier

Jake Sonnett pedaled his paper route the way he always did — steady, thoughtful, humming under his breath as the town began to awaken to a new day. The apartment building on Royal Avenue adjoining Nick's Good Food Diner was his last stop, a three-story structure with peeling paint and a stairwell that always smelled faintly of boiled cabbage.

He disliked delivering there. Folks were friendly enough, but the old building had a way of communicating deterioration.

A car he didn't recognize was parked behind the building — a dark sedan with a lot of rust. And upstairs, in Apartment 2B, a man's voice was raised, sharp and angry, cutting through the thin walls.

Jake paused at the bottom of the stairs, one foot on the ground, listening.

"…I said I want my money now!"

Another voice answered — lower, rougher, with an edge that made Jake's stomach tighten.

"You'll get paid when I get paid. Not before."

Jake swallowed. He wasn't supposed to linger. His mother always said, "Deliver the paper and come straight home." But something in the tone of those voices rooted him to the spot.

He climbed the stairs quietly, the newspapers under his arm rustling. As he reached the landing, the argument sharpened.

"You listen to me," the rough voice growled. "You'll get paid when I get paid. Take it or leave it!"

A pause. Then:

"It's an antique drawing, for God's sake. Worth more than you know."

Jake froze.

Inside the apartment, a chair scraped.

A crash. A scuffle. A grunt of pain.

Jake stepped back instinctively, but his foot hit the metal stair rail with a sharp clang.

Inside the apartment, Pike shouted, "You're not going to snitch on me!"

The shot cracked through the apartment like the crack of a whip.

Jake's whole body went cold.

He didn't wait to hear more. He bolted down the stairs, leaped onto his bike, and pedaled to the Texaco station on the corner.

An attendant was checking under the hood of a car parked by the pumps. Jake, shaking almost uncontrollably, yelled, "Did you hear it? Somebody just shot somebody in the apartment building!" pointing toward the building.

"Are you sure, son?" the attendant said as he stood up with an oil dipstick in his hand.

"Yes,a police car sir. I heard two guys arguing and then the shot."

The attendant could see that the boy was scared, and he needed to take seriously what he was saying.

"Okay, son. Just settle down. You come with me and wait inside the station while I call the cops."

In a very few minutes, a police car rolled up to the Texaco station, lights off but moving fast. Two officers jumped out—men Jake recognized from seeing them around town—and the attendant hurried over to explain what he'd heard.

"Kid says there was an argument and then a shot," the attendant said, jerking his thumb toward Jake. "Probably a domestic quarrel, but it sounded bad enough to call you."

One of the officers crouched slightly to meet Jake's eyes. "Which apartment, son?"

Jake swallowed. "Two-B," he said, his voice steadier now but still thin around the edges.

That was all they needed. The officers exchanged a quick look, then ran toward the building, guns drawn, disappearing up the stairwell.

Jake stayed where he was, hugging his elbows, the tremor in his hands slowly easing. The longer he stood there, the more the shock drained away, replaced by a different kind of worry—he was supposed to be home soon, supposed to get ready for school, supposed to pretend this morning was like any other. His bike leaned against the pump, front wheel still spinning from how fast he'd ridden.

Minutes passed. It felt like a long time.

Finally, one of the policemen came back out, walking briskly to the patrol car. He picked up the radio mic, turning slightly away from Jake and the attendant, but not enough to hide the words.

"Dispatch, this is Unit Three. We've got an apparent suicide at 575 North Royal," he said. "We'll need assistance and a full investigation team."

Jake's stomach dropped. Suicide. That wasn't what he'd heard. That wasn't what it sounded like at all.

He stood very still, the morning suddenly too bright, too ordinary for what he'd just witnessed.

Across the street, the front door of The Warren Sentinel swung open and Ted Bromfield—editor, reporter, photographer, and half the newspaper staff—stepped out with his camera slung around his neck. He shaded his eyes, spotted the police car, and hurried across the street, his tie flapping behind him.

"What's going on?" he called, already reaching for the focus ring on his camera.

One of the officers held up a hand. "Stand back, Ted. We're checking it out."

Ted didn't argue—just hovered nearby, notebook ready, the way he always did when something worth printing might be unfolding.

The other officer turned to Jake. "Son, we need your name."

Jake swallowed. "Jake Sonnett."

"Address?"

"Eight West Fifth Street – just a block away."

The officer wrote quickly, then added, "Phone number?"

Jake recited it, his voice steadier now, though his hands still trembled at his sides.

"All right," the officer said, tucking the notebook away. "You can go on home. We'll be in touch if we need anything else."

Jake nodded, relief and exhaustion washing over him at the same time. If the police had his name, if they were handling it, then maybe—maybe—he could just let it go. They'd figure out what happened. They always did. He was just a kid who'd been in the wrong place at the wrong time.

He climbed onto his bike, the seat still warm from his frantic ride earlier. As he pushed off and began pedaling toward home, he tried to shove the whole horrible incident out of his mind—the arguing voices and the gunshot he could still hear echoing in his head. He had to get home, had to get ready for school, had to pretend this morning was like any other.

As he reached the end of the block, the distant wail of a siren rose behind him and then cut off abruptly. Jake glanced over his shoulder just in time to see a second police car pull up to the curb outside the apartment building. Two more officers stepped out—one carrying a small canvas kit, the other already pulling on thin rubber gloves.

They spoke briefly with the first officer, their voices low and businesslike, then headed into the building without so much as a glance toward Jake or Ted Bromfield, who was still scribbling notes by the patrol car. Whatever was happening inside, it was now officially more than a routine call.

Jake kept pedaling, the scene shrinking behind him. His hands were steadier now, though his stomach still felt hollow. The police had his name, his address, his phone number. They would figure it out. They always did. He was just a kid who'd heard something he wished he hadn't.

He rounded the corner toward home, telling himself he needed to forget the whole thing—erase it from his mind before school, before breakfast, before it became something too big to carry.

He never found out what really happened. The police never called.

And as the days passed, the memory of that morning settled into a quiet corner of his mind—something he told himself to forget, even though he never really could.

The Framed Drawing

Terry Miller decided to take the morning off work—there were some important things he had to do. He drove to the Bank of Warren, withdrew two hundred dollars in four crisp fifties, and slipped them into his wallet. Then he headed straight for the pawn shop.

The front door was locked. The CLOSED sign hung crookedly in the window.

He knocked. Hard and repeatedly.

For a moment, nothing happened. Then he heard movement—hurried, uneven—coming from the back of the store. A shadow flickered behind the counter glass.

Wally Harlan appeared, rushing forward, breathing hard. His thick glasses were slightly askew, and his shirt was untucked on one side as if he'd thrown it back on in a hurry. His hands—those quick, powerful boxer's hands—were trembling just enough to notice. One knuckle was reddened, scraped, as though it had struck something or someone.

For a split second—barely long enough to register—Terry saw a look of what he thought was annoyance in Harlan's eyes.

Then it was gone, replaced by the usual guarded scowl.

Harlan unlocked the door with a jerk. "We're not open yet," he muttered, trying to straighten his glasses and tuck in his shirt at the same time.

Terry stepped inside anyway. "Won't take long."

Harlan hesitated—just a flicker—but enough to show he wasn't in the mood for company. Or questions.

Terry kept his voice even, almost conversational. "I've got people who can vouch for me. Upstanding folks. Laura Virginia Hale, Mrs. Norton. A couple others. They all saw the drawing in my hands before it went missing."

Harlan's jaw tightened. His scraped knuckle twitched against the counter. "Doesn't mean it's yours."

"It does," Terry said, still calm. "And they'll say so. Every one of them."

For a moment, Harlan looked like a man calculating the cost of a fight he didn't want. His eyes darted toward the back room—just for a heartbeat—before snapping back to Terry.

Terry reached into his wallet and laid a crisp fifty on the counter. "I'm willing to make it right. Fifty dollars."

Harlan snorted. "Fifty? I was gonna put it in a nice frame. Good wood. Glass. That's a hundred and fifty right there."

Terry paused. A frame. He hadn't thought of that. A frame would protect the drawing—keep it from folding, tearing, getting lost again. It was actually a good idea.

He pulled out another bill. "A hundred."

Harlan's eyes flicked to the money. His fingers twitched—those quick, powerful boxer's hands that earlier had wrenched a man's gun back toward him before he fired. In a blink, Harlan scooped up the bills before Terry even registered the movement.

"Sold," Harlan said, voice low.

He slid the bills into his pocket, then added, "I'll have it framed and ready for you by noon."

"I'll wait," Terry said.

Harlan frowned. "Noon. I said noon. Come back then."

"Frame it now while I wait," Terry repeated, calm and immovable.

For a second, Harlan just stared at him, his jaw working. He looked toward the back room as if hoping for a way to escape that wasn't there.

"Fine," he muttered. "Fine. Give me a minute."

He disappeared into the back, and Terry heard him rummaging—hurried, uneven, nothing like the smooth, confident movements of a man who knew every inch of his shop. Glass clinked. A frame thumped onto a workbench. A muttered curse floated out, followed by the sharp snap of a staple gun.

After several tense minutes, Harlan reappeared holding the drawing in a simple but sturdy frame. The glass was slightly smudged from his unsteady hands, but the work was solid.

Terry took it carefully, relief washing through him as he tucked it under his arm.

"Thanks," he said, turning toward the door.

But as he stepped outside, the weight of the frame pressed against his ribs, and another thought rose in him—sharp, insistent, impossible to ignore.

There was more he had to do.

He drove straight to Parkway Chevrolet, the framed drawing riding on the seat beside him like something fragile and important. The big plate-glass windows of the showroom flashed sunlight as he pulled in, rows of gleaming cars lined up like chrome-plated promises.

He tucked the frame under his arm and went inside.

"Morning, Terry!" Rice Mathews, the owner, called from behind a desk near the front, his tie loose, his grin wide and automatic. "What brings you in? Looking to trade up?"

"Not today, Rice," Terry said, managing a small smile. "I need to see Bill Sonnett for a moment. Is he busy?"

Rice glanced toward a small glass-walled office off the showroom. A brass nameplate on the door read: Bill Sonnett, Sales Manager.

"He's on the phone," Rice said. "But go on over. He'll be done in a minute."

Terry nodded and walked across the polished floor, the new car smell thick in the air. He paused outside Bill's office. Through the glass, he could see Bill leaning back in his chair, phone to his ear, one hand absently tapping a pencil against a stack of papers.

Terry shifted the frame under his arm and let his eyes wander over the cars in the showroom—shiny Impalas, a bright red Corvette that looked like it belonged in a magazine, not in Warren County. For a moment he let himself daydream—about open roads, about leaving town, about a life where drawings didn't get stolen and pawned.

The office door clicked open.

Bill stepped out, hanging up the phone as he did. "Terry," he said, extending his hand. "Good to see you. What can I do for you?"

They shook hands. Terry nodded toward the frame. "I wanted to show you this."

He brought the drawing out from under his arm and held it up. The simple frame made it look more finished, more real—like something that belonged on a wall instead of in a folder.

"I had it framed," Terry said. "Sorry it took me so long to get back to you. Things got…complicated."

Bill studied the drawing for a moment, his expression softening. "It looks good," he said. "Real good."

Terry took a breath. "If it's okay with you, I'd still like Jake to copy it. I haven't changed my mind about that."

He met Bill's eyes, the framed drawing between them like a quiet, serious promise.

Bill studied the framed drawing a moment longer, then nodded. "Jake'll be glad to work on it. I can take it home with me and have him start after school."

Terry shifted the frame under his arm. "If it's all the same to you, I'd rather bring it by myself. About five o'clock?"

Bill smiled. "Five works just fine."

He handed the drawing back to Terry, then leaned against the doorframe, his tone softening. "You know, that boy of mine… he's a real daydreamer. He has more talent than I ever had at his age, but sometimes I worry he spends too much time in his own little world." He sighed. "He's got his paper route, and he and his brother walk to school, but outside of that he doesn't do much that gets him moving. Maybe he just needs more physical activity."

Terry nodded. "When I was your son's age, my dad used to take me duckpin bowling. Any night but Thursday—teams had the lanes then. Little balls, easy for a kid to handle. I wasn't any good, but it was fun exercise. Kept me out of trouble. Funny thing is, today I'm on a team."

Bill's eyes brightened. "Bowling. Now that's not a bad idea. He might go for that."

"Worth a try," Terry said.

They walked together toward the front doors, the smell of new cars and wax giving way to the cool morning air outside. Bill glanced at Terry's pickup parked near the curb.

"You know," he said, half-teasing, half-serious, "that truck of yours is about ready for retirement. We've got some great deals right now. I could set you up with something that won't rattle your teeth loose."

Terry laughed. "Maybe one day."

"Just say the word," Bill said, giving the fender an affectionate tap as they passed.

Terry nodded, the framed drawing tucked securely under his arm. He had what he came for. And now, with the next step waiting for him at four o'clock, he felt the weight of the morning shift again.

There was still something he needed to do before then.

Terry's next stop was Laura Virginia Hale's house. It was a promise he needed to keep. He had told her he'd come back, and he wasn't the kind of man to let a promise drift.

Mrs. Pruitt let him in, and Laura Virginia looked up from her chair with that bright, bird-like alertness she always had when something interesting was afoot.

"Well now," she said, smiling. "You've brought it back."

Terry held up the frame. "I had it put under glass. Thought it ought to be protected."

She leaned forward, studying it with the same reverence she gave to old photographs and family Bibles. "It's even lovelier this way. What did Mrs. Norton say?"

"That she doesn't think it's a sampler at all," Terry said. "She thinks it's a map—one that's pretending to be a sampler."

Laura Virginia's eyebrows lifted. "A map. Yes… yes, I can see that. The spacing, the odd little flourishes. It always felt like it was hiding something."

"There's more," Terry said. "Mrs. Norton found a letter. Tucked inside an old book from the Marigold estate. Civil War era, she thinks. She's written to the University of Virginia about it."

Laura Virginia sat back, her expression sharpening with interest. "The Marigolds again. That family never did anything halfway. Secrets piled on secrets."

Terry smiled faintly. "Seems that way."

Laura Virginia fixed her gaze on the frame, her eyes narrowing with that far-off look she got when memory and intuition braided together.

"You know, Terry… the Marigolds were a family of secrets. Always have been."

Terry smiled politely. "Most old families are."

She shook her head. "Not like them. One of the daughters—lived to be a hundred and one. Never married. Taught school for a few years, then withdrew from the world. Became… well, reclusive isn't quite the word. She was *watchful.* Like she knew something the rest of us didn't."

Terry leaned in a little. "What was mysterious about her?"

"Oh, everything." Laura Virginia's voice dropped, almost conspiratorial. "There were rumors she'd been a spy in the War Between the States. She's buried right up there in Prospect Hill Cemetery."

Terry felt a small chill. "What was her name, by chance?"

Laura Virginia's eyes softened, almost fond. "Alethea Marigold."

The name in Mrs. Norton's letter. The name hinted at in the drawing's strange geometry. A.M.

He let this settle in him, heavy and significant.

Terry realized he had to hurry to work. He thanked Laura Virginia and stepped out into the bright morning; the framed drawing tucked under his arm. As he walked to his truck, the name she'd spoken kept circling in his mind like a moth around a porch light.

Alethea Marigold. Lived to be 101. Never married. Taught school, then withdrew from the world. Rumored spy. Keeper of secrets. A.M.

The name that was on Mrs. Norton's letter. The very same initials that whispered from the corner of the drawing.

He set the frame carefully on the seat beside him and drove toward the plant. The road felt different now—like he was moving through a story he hadn't realized he was part of until this morning.

By the time he pulled into the parking lot, he felt a small, steady satisfaction. He'd kept his promise to Laura Virginia. He'd learned something real—something that made the drawing feel heavier, more important.

But once he clocked in, the satisfaction didn't help him focus.

He stood at his station staring at a half-assembled part, realizing he'd been holding the same wrench for longer than made sense. The noise of the plant—usually a kind of background rhythm he could settle into—felt distant, muffled, like he was underwater.

Alethea Marigold. A map disguised as a sampler. A letter hidden in a book. A woman who carried secrets through a war and lived long enough to bury them.

Terry tried to shake it off, tried to focus on the job in front of him, but the morning clung to him like a shadow he couldn't quite step out of.

The Plan

Professor Daniel Whitmore stepped into Samuel's Library, the rattling of the open sign on the door sounding loud in the quiet of the old house. He paused just inside, letting his eyes adjust to the warm, late-afternoon light that filtered through the tall front windows. He was a man in his early forties, trim but slightly stooped from years bent over archives, with a thoughtful, almost courtly way of carrying himself. His suit was neat but travel-creased, his tie a little off-center, and his hair—dark with a premature streak of silver—had clearly lost a battle with the mountain breeze outside. There was something earnest in his face, something that suggested he lived more in the world of ideas than in the world of errands and timetables.

"Good afternoon," he said, offering a polite, slightly self-conscious smile to the woman sitting behind the circulation desk. "Are you Mrs. Eleanor Norton?"

"I am," she replied, curious but welcoming. "How can I help you?"

"I'm Daniel Whitmore," he said. "From the University of Virginia. And I owe you an apology for arriving unannounced. I should have called first, but your letter came in my mail just this morning. After reading it, I thought it best to come straight here."

Recognition warmed her expression. "Professor Whitmore. Well—this is a pleasant surprise. I wasn't sure how long it might take for that letter to find the right person."

"It found me," he said. "And your inquiry was forwarded directly to my office. I wanted to speak with you about the document you found."

Eleanor nodded and reached beneath the counter. "I have it right here." She unfolded a protective sleeve and slid out the letter—aged paper, careful handwriting, the faintest scent of cedar and dust. “It turned up in a donated book last week from the Marigold estate.”

Whitmore leaned in, studying the ink, the slant of the script, the peculiar phrasing. Intrigue flickered across his features. “This is… quite something,” he murmured. “But I’ll need to do a bit of research before I can give you a proper opinion. The language and style of writing suggest a particular period, but I’d like to confirm my suspicions.”

“Of course,” Eleanor said. “I didn’t expect an instant verdict.”

She hesitated, then added, “And there’s something else. A drawing.”

Whitmore’s attention sharpened. “A drawing?”

“One of our patrons—Terry Miller’s his name—brought it in Saturday morning. I told him it appears to be a kind of map disguised as a sampler. Quite old. Quite unusual. It had a design of curving vines crisscrossing through the center and two sets of initials, C.N. and A.M.”

Whitmore blinked. “Mrs. Norton… I believe I’ve seen that drawing.”

“Oh?”

“At the pawn shop on Main Street. The owner showed it to me and quoted a price—five hundred dollars. Far too much for my small budget.”

Eleanor’s brows rose. “Well, that’s strange. Terry’s drawing didn’t come from a shop. He told me it came from the Marigold estate—the same place as the letter.”

Whitmore sensed a connection forming, faint but undeniable.

"Both items from the same estate," he murmured. "That's… significant."

"I thought so too," she said gently. "That's why I reached out to the University."

"I'd very much like to see the drawing Terry brought you," Whitmore said. "If he's willing."

"I'm sure he is," she said. "But he works during the day. I'll call him this evening and see if he can be available tomorrow sometime after five o'clock at the earliest. Would that work for you?"

"Of course," Whitmore said. "Tuesday, five o'clock here?"

"That would suit me fine. I'm anxious to have you see Terry's drawing."

"Thank you, Mrs. Norton. Truly."

She gave him a small, knowing smile. "These old things have a way of choosing their moment to be understood."

Whitmore stepped back toward the lobby, the hush of the library settling around him like dust in a sunbeam.

Something in Front Royal was beginning to stir.

A Happy Creek Morning

Eddie Combs eased the back door shut with all the care he could muster. The hinges gave a soft whine, but the sound was swallowed by the deeper rumble of his father's snoring drifting from the living room couch. Eddie paused on the porch, listening. Nothing changed. His father was still dead to the world, one arm dangling toward the floor, an empty bottle glinting on its side beneath the coffee table.

Good. If the old man woke and found Eddie home on a school morning, there'd be hell to pay.

Eddie slipped down the steps, wheeled his bike out from behind the oil tank, and pushed it to the alley before daring to climb on. Only when he reached the end of the block did he let out the breath he'd been holding.

The morning was cool and bright; the kind of spring day that made the whole town smell like damp earth and new leaves. Eddie pedaled fast, his back wheel giving its familiar squeak every third turn. He liked the sound — it made him feel as though he was outrunning something.

Carson's Eastside Grocery sat at the corner of Sixth Street and Manassas Avenue, its screen door patched twice over and the Coca-Cola sign out front faded to a soft pink. Eddie leaned his bike against the wall and pushed inside.

The store smelled of coffee grounds, old wood, and the sweet tang of oranges stacked in a wooden crate. Mr. Carson stood behind the counter, sorting receipts with the slow, steady movements of a man who'd been doing the same thing since before Eddie was born.

"Mornin', Eddie," he said without looking up. "You're out early."

Eddie squared his shoulders, trying to look older than sixteen. "Pack of Marlboros," he said, voice pitched low.

Mr. Carson finally looked at him — not unkindly, but with the weary patience of someone who'd seen this play out before. "You're not old enough to buy cigarettes, son."

Eddie scowled. "Come on. Nobody's gonna know."

"I'll know," Carson said. "And so will your father when he smells you. And speaking of him — why aren't you in school?"

"Teacher workday," Eddie muttered.

Carson raised an eyebrow. "Funny. My niece teaches at the middle school. She didn't mention any workday."

Eddie's ears burned. He shifted tactics. "Fine. I'll take a Twinkie and a bottle of pop."

Carson rang them up.

Eddie quickly grabbed a pack of matches, slapped his coins on the counter, and stuffed the change into his pocket. He didn't look back as he rushed out the door.

Behind the store, hidden between the trash cans and a patch of scrubby bushes, he tore open the Twinkie wrapper with his teeth. The cake was squished, but he devoured it in three bites, washing it down with grape pop. The sugar hit him fast, warm and bright.

He sat for a moment, listening to the hum of morning traffic going up and down Sixth Street. The world felt wide open when he wasn't stuck behind a school desk.

He hopped back on his bike and pedaled toward the Sinclair station at the edge of town. The green dinosaur sign creaked in the breeze, and the smell of gasoline hung thick in the air. Eddie leaned his bike against the ice chest and slipped inside.

The cigarette machine stood in the corner, humming faintly. Eddie fed in two quarters one by one, glancing over his shoulder. The attendant was outside pumping gas and more interested in chatting with the pretty blond behind the wheel than watching Eddie. Eddie pulled the lever.

A pack of Marlboros dropped with a satisfying clunk.

He pocketed them and rode off again, this time toward Happy Creek.

The creek ran behind a stretch of woods past Bing Crosby Stadium, a place kids used for fishing, skipping rocks, and hiding from whatever they didn't want to face. Eddie ditched his bike in the tall grass and pushed through the underbrush until he found his usual spot — a hollow between two sycamores where the branches formed a kind of leafy ceiling.

He sat cross-legged, tore open the cigarette pack, and lit one. The first drag made him cough, but he forced himself to keep going, imagining how cool he must look, smoke curling around him like he was a movie heartthrob.

The creek burbled softly nearby. Sunlight flickered through the leaves. A dragonfly hovered over the water, wings catching the light like stained glass.

Eddie leaned back against the tree and let his mind wander.

Saturday's "find" — that strange drawing he'd spotted in the ditch along Happy Creek Road — had been the most exciting thing to happen in months. Maybe years. He could still picture it: the folded paper, the looping lines, the initials in the corners. He hadn't understood it, but Mr.

Harlan at the pawn shop had. The man's eyes had gone sharp the moment Eddie unfolded it on the counter.

"Five dollars," Harlan had said, already reaching into his cash drawer.

Five dollars. More money than Eddie usually saw at once.

And if he could find one thing like that, he could find another.

He took another drag, squinting through the smoke.

Maybe he'd go back out there. Maybe he'd poke around the edges of the property. Maybe he'd find something worth money. Something worth more than money.

The thought warmed him more than the cigarette.

He jumped back on his bike and sped toward the pawn shop.

Eddie pushed open the pawn shop door, the bell giving a thin, nervous jangle. The lights were dimmer than usual, and the air felt close, as if the place had been shut tight for hours.

From the back room came a sharp rustle, then Harlan appeared — hair mussed, shirt untucked, a sheen of sweat still clinging to his temples. His eyes flicked to the street behind Eddie before settling on the boy with a look that was far from friendly.

"What're you doing here?" Harlan snapped. "Ain't you supposed to be in school?"

Eddie blinked. "It's lunch period. I just wanted to—"

"Well, lunch is over. Go on. Out." Harlan waved him toward the door with a jerky, impatient motion. "I ain't got time for kids hangin' around today."

Eddie frowned. "I just wanted to see if you still had that—"

"I said *out.*" Harlan stepped closer, lowering his voice to a harsh whisper. "You want me to call the truancy officer? Because I will. I'll have him down here in five minutes."

Eddie stiffened. "I didn't do nothin'."

"Then don't start." Harlan's gaze darted again toward the back room — too quick, too nervous — and Eddie felt a prickle of unease. "Now get on home before I make that call."

Eddie backed toward the door, confused and a little shaken. He stepped outside. Behind him, Harlan locked the door — actually locked it — and yanked the shade down with a snap.

Eddie stood on the sidewalk for a moment, staring at the closed shopfront.

He wasn't ready to go home. Not with his father there. Not with the day still wide open.

So he headed west on Main toward the Murphy Theater.

The theater's back door was easy to jimmy — Eddie had learned that last summer. He slipped inside the dim hallway, the smell of stale popcorn and floor polish wrapping around him like a blanket. The manager, Mr. Dugan, was out front somewhere, vacuuming and muttering to himself.

Eddie crept up the aisle and slid into the back row, sinking low in the seat. If he stayed quiet, he could hide out here till noon. Maybe longer.

The vacuum roared. Dugan's voice rose above it, grousing about "pigs" and "filthy animals" and "things no decent person should leave under a seat." Eddie smirked. He'd heard it all before.

He lit a cigarette, cupping the flame with his hand. The smoke curled upward, sweet and sharp. And then—

The vacuum snapped off.

The sound of a sniff. Another.

"Who's back there?" Dugan barked. Eddie froze.

Footsteps pounded up the aisle.

Dugan's face appeared out of the dim, red-eyed and furious. "You again! Out! And if I catch you sneakin' in here one more time, I'm callin' your father!"

Eddie bolted, slipping past him and out the back door before the man could grab him.

He didn't stop running until he reached the alley. His heart hammered. The cigarette was gone, dropped somewhere in the scramble.

He leaned against the wall, catching his breath. Fine. The theater was out. He'd kill time somewhere else.

Maybe near the school. If he hung around the edge of the parking lot, nobody would notice him. He could hide his bike in the tall grass and come back later to retrieve it. And when the bell rang and kids poured out, he could blend right in, like he'd been there all along.

Eddie swung onto his bike and pedaled toward Warren County High, the squeak of his back wheel keeping time with the restless beat of his thoughts.

He wasn't going home. Not yet. Not until the day was safely behind him.

A Father's Concern

The back door creaked open just as Jeanie was setting two plates on the kitchen table. Bill stepped inside, loosening his tie and rubbing the back of his neck as if the morning had been longer than it ought to be.

"You're home early," Jeanie said, smiling as she wiped her hands on a dish towel.

"Figured I'd take off work a bit early and see my best girl," Bill said, leaning in to kiss her cheek. "And get something to eat before I fall over."

"You're in luck," she said. "Chicken salad and some of your dad's delicious tomatoes."

Bill removed his jacket and adjusted it on the back of his chair. He sat down, exhaling as though the chair had been saving that spot just for him.

"It's been a busy day. Been on the phone most of the morning closing a big deal. By the way, Terry Miller stopped by the dealership earlier," he said, reaching for his fork. "Brought that drawing he wants Jake to copy. Had it framed and everything."

Jeanie raised her eyebrows. "Framed? My, he's taking this seriously."

"He is," Bill said. "And he's going to drop by around five. I told him Jake could work on it this evening if he got all his homework done first."

Jeanie nodded thoughtfully. "Maybe we should invite him to stay for dinner. He's been good to Jake. And he's alone too much for a young man."

Bill smiled at that — the gentle way she always looked out for people. "I think he'd like that."

They ate for a moment in comfortable silence, the kind that comes from years of knowing each other's rhythms. Outside, the noon sun slanted across the yard, catching the laundry on the line and making it glow like small white flags.

"So," Bill said between bites, "we ought to talk about summer vacation."

Jeanie brightened. "I've been thinking about that too. The boys are already counting the days."

"I was thinking Sherando Lake," Bill said. "Camping, hiking, swimming. About two hours' drive."

"And fishing," Jeanie added. "Jake would love that. Emmett too, though he'll probably scare every fish in Virginia."

Bill chuckled. "That's half the fun."

"But…" Jeanie tapped her fingers lightly on the table. "Clara told me that she and her brood are going to Rehoboth Beach this summer. That's only three and a half hours. Ocean waves, boardwalk, real beds. No camping, but it might be nice to have a little comfort."

Bill nodded. "True. But Sherando's quieter. More our speed. And cheaper."

She studied him for a moment. "You're leaning toward Sherando."

"I am," he admitted. "Feels like the right kind of summer for us."

Jeanie smiled softly. "Then Sherando it is — at least for now. When should we tell the boys?"

"Hold off until I have a chance to firm up my vacation days."

Bill finished his sandwich, then hesitated, a more serious look settling over him.

"Jeanie… I'm worried about Jake."

Her face softened. "What's going on?"

"It's not that anything happened," Bill said. "It's the way he's been drifting off. He'll be right in the middle of something and suddenly he's somewhere else entirely. Like he loses track of the moment. It's more than daydreaming—almost like he blanks out for a second. I don't want to ignore it."

Jeanie nodded slowly. "I've noticed it too. He goes deep inside his head. He feels things intensely, and sometimes it pulls him away from the world around him."

"That's why I'm going to call the school this afternoon," Bill said. "Set up a meeting with his teacher. Just to get a sense of where he is."

"I think that's wise," Jeanie said. "He needs guidance. And he needs you."

"Truth is, I remember drifting a bit myself at his age. Took me a while to find my footing."

Bill stood, kissed her forehead, and reached for his jacket. "I'll be home on time tonight. And we'll have Terry for dinner if he'll stay."

"He will," Jeanie said with quiet certainty. "People don't turn down a Sonnett supper."

Jeanie reached up and straightened the knot of his tie without thinking, the way she had since their first year of marriage.

Bill grinned, stepped out into the bright afternoon, and headed back to the car dealership— carrying with him the steady resolve of a father determined to keep his family on solid ground.

The Copy

Terry pulled into the Sonnetts' driveway just as the porch light blinked on, casting a warm circle across the steps. The house had that settled, welcoming glow that always made him feel as if he were stepping into a place where the world still made sense. Bill opened the door before Terry could knock.

"Evenin', Terry. Come on in. Jake's been pacing like a cat on a hot stove."

Jake appeared behind his father, eyes bright. "Did you bring it?"

Terry held up the framed drawing. "Right here."

Jake ushered him straight to the kitchen table, already cleared except for his new drawing pad, a ruler, a freshly sharpened pencil, and a bottle of Higgins ink with the cork still in place. Jeanie wiped her hands on a dish towel and smiled.

"He's been waiting all afternoon."

Jake handled the drawing with reverence, studying the lines, the shading, the way the old paper had mellowed with age. "It's beautiful," he murmured. "I'll take real good care of it."

"You just do your best," Terry said. "Mrs. Norton said you were the man for the job."

Jeanie poured Terry a cup of coffee and set it beside him. "Long day at work?"

Terry nodded, then his face brightened. "It was, but something good happened right after. The librarian called me — said she'd been thinking about an old letter she has and my drawing. She's arranged for me to meet with her and an expert on old documents tomorrow afternoon."

Bill let out a low whistle. "Well now, that sounds promising."

"Sure does," Terry said. "I don't know what they'll say, but… it feels like things are finally moving."

Jeanie smiled warmly. "You deserve some good news."

Terry glanced at Jake. "And having this copy made — that's part of it. Feels like everything's lining up."

Jake straightened a little at that. He set the drawing pad beside the original and began marking faint guide points with his pencil, measuring carefully. His concentration was absolute — the kind that made the room fall into a hush around him.

Bill leaned toward Terry. "He gets that from his mother's side," he whispered. "I can't draw a straight line with a ruler."

Jeanie swatted him lightly with the towel. "You hush."

Jake dipped the pen, touched it to the paper, and began. The first strokes were slow and deliberate, but steady. The room seemed to settle into a shared breath as the lines took shape — the same curves, the same shadows, only smaller and cleaner, alive again under Jake's hand.

By the time Jeanie called them to dinner, Jake had finished the entire outline. He held it up, ink still drying.

"Jake… that's perfect," Terry said, shaking his head in disbelief.

Jake flushed with pride. "I'll finish the shading after dinner. I want it to be just right."

Jeanie announced that dinner was ready and everyone gathered around the table — roast chicken, mashed potatoes, green beans with bacon. The kind of meal that made a man forget the world outside.

Terry commented, "You know, it's nice that you folks give thanks before you eat. Sometimes I miss those old ways. Folks back then gave thanks and had better manners. Kids said 'sir' and 'ma'am.' People looked out for each other."

Jeanie raised an eyebrow. "People still do."

"Sure," Bill said, "but the world's changing fast. New gadgets, new ideas. Hard to keep up. And I sell cars — there's a new model every year. Can't fight progress."

Terry nodded slowly. "Maybe we don't have to fight it. Maybe the trick is to welcome what's good and hold on to what matters."

Jeanie smiled at that. "I believe it begins and ends with the family. If the home is steady, the world can change all it wants."

Bill tapped his fork on the table. "That's the truth."

Jake, still glowing from his work, added quietly, "Some things shouldn't change. Like people helping each other."

Terry looked at him — really looked — and felt something settle in his chest. A sense of rightness. Of belonging. Of the old ways living on in small, steady acts.

When dinner was over and the dishes were cleared, Jake returned to the table and finished the shading with the same careful attention he'd given the outline. When he finally lifted the pen and set it aside, he held the drawing up with both hands.

"What do you think?" he asked.

Terry leaned in. The copy was flawless — every curve, every shadow, every delicate line faithfully rendered. Only the size and the fresh white paper gave it away.

"Jake," he said softly, "that's perfect. Absolutely perfect. And fast too."

Jake grinned, a little embarrassed but glowing all the same.

Terry reached into his wallet and pulled out a crisp ten-dollar bill. "This is for your work."

Jake's eyes widened. "Wow! Thanks!" He looked at the bill as if it might float away. "I guess that makes me a professional artist now."

Bill chuckled from the doorway. "Looks that way to me."

Jeanie smiled. "Every professional has to start somewhere."

Jake tucked the bill carefully into his pocket, still grinning.

"And how do you plan to spend it?" Terry asked.

"I know exactly where I'll spend it," Jake answered. "Right in Mr. Zunka's store for more art supplies."

Terry smiled and rolled Jake's copy, slipping a rubber band around it. Holding the two drawings — one framed and the other rolled, the fragile past and the fresh new version — he felt a strange, buoyant sense of blessing. As if the world had handed him a small sign that things might finally be turning his way.

He thanked them all again, stepped out into the cool night air, and headed toward his truck feeling lighter than he had in a long time. As he opened the door, he said to himself, “If I ever have a family, I want it to be exactly like the Sonnetts.”

The Truth of the Drawing

Samuel's Library had once been an eight-room home, and it still felt like one after closing for the day. Norton led Whitmore and Terry down the narrow central hallway, past the former parlor and sitting room, to a small ground-floor room tucked into the back corner of the house.

"This will give us privacy," she said, unlocking the door.

The room was plain but serviceable: a long, well-worn table that hosted board meetings, four mismatched chairs, and a single shaded lamp that cast a warm circle of light across the tabletop. The rest of the room fell into gentle shadow.

Terry stepped inside, holding the framed drawing with both hands. "I've been nervous carrying this around all day," he admitted.

Whitmore set his coat neatly over a chair. "Let's have a look."

Norton crossed to a small cabinet and withdrew the letter from Charles to Alethea, still in its protective sleeve. She placed it on the table with quiet care. "I've kept it locked up," she said. "Didn't want to risk anything happening to it."

Terry laid the framed drawing beside it. "I had it framed," he said. "Seemed like the right thing to do."

Whitmore nodded approvingly. "A sensible choice."

He removed a pair of white cotton gloves from his brief case and put them on.

"May I remove it from the frame?" he asked, looking up at Terry.

"Do you have to?" Terry asked.

"It will be necessary. I know what I'm doing," the professor said.

"Okay," Terry said, though his voice wavered.

Whitmore worked slowly, loosening the backing with practiced fingers. "Old paper can be temperamental," he murmured. "But this frame was done well."

He eased the drawing free and set it gently on the table. For a long moment, the three of them simply looked at it. The room felt smaller, as though the past had drawn its chair up to the table with them.

Whitmore leaned in, using a magnifier to study the ink lines, the shading, the faint irregularities that only time could produce. He didn't touch it — only hovered a few inches above it.

Norton watched him closely. Terry held his breath.

Whitmore took his time. Norton and Terry waited.

And waited.

At last, Whitmore spoke. "The hand is the same. The flourishes, the pressure, the way the lines pull toward the left. The penwork is authentic to the time. All things considered, my conclusion is this drawing is unquestionably authentic."

Terry let out a shaky exhale. "So it really is… something."

"It is," Whitmore said. "And paired with the letter, it becomes even more significant."

"But is it a design for a sampler or a map?" Terry asked.

The professor rubbed his chin. "If it's a map, it's not one that wants to be read quickly. And if it's a sampler, it's the strangest one I've ever seen."

He lifted the letter next, examining the slant of the script. "The Charles in this letter was Charles Nation. An army captain and regimental commander. Killed in the war. A promising young man — and deeply attached to Alethea."

Norton's expression softened. "Poor girl."

Whitmore nodded. "She taught school for a short time — a spinster schoolmarm, the records say. Even taught porcelain painting to the girls in town." He gave a faint, knowing smile. "A popular pastime then."

Terry leaned forward. "What happened to her?"

"The story is she never recovered from losing Charles," Whitmore said quietly. "Turned to spiritualism, as many grieving women did after the war. Held seances up there in the mansion. Lived to be 101, but by all accounts she carried her sorrow to the very end of her long life."

"Do you know the year she died?" Mrs. Norton asked.

"1940. She is buried in the family plot on the estate," Professor Whitmore answered.

Terry frowned slightly. "Are you sure about that?"

Whitmore looked up. "Quite sure. There's a tombstone with her name on it in the Marigold plot."

"That's strange," Terry said. "I was told she's buried in Prospect Hill Cemetery."

Whitmore considered this. "There may be a story behind that. Families sometimes placed memorial stones in more than one location. Or someone may have misremembered. But the stone on the estate is real."

He studied Terry a moment. "Have you ever been inside the old house?"

"Never inside," Terry said. "Just seen it from the road."

Whitmore nodded. "I need to go up there in the next few days to photograph and catalog a few things. If you could meet me up there Saturday morning, say around ten, I'll give you a tour of the house and the grounds. It might help you appreciate the value of your drawing — to see the place where it was created."

Terry's face lit. "I'd like that. I really would. Thank you, Professor."

"My pleasure," Whitmore said. "It's a remarkable place."

The room fell silent — not heavy, but respectful.

Whitmore cleared his throat. "There are four drawings in this series. I've seen the other three. This one"—he pointed to Terry's drawing—"is the missing piece."

Terry blinked. "Missing?"

"And because of that — and because of the letter — I estimate that this one alone is worth around ten thousand dollars."

Norton drew in a sharp breath. Terry stared at the drawing as though it might vanish.

Whitmore folded his hands. "It's a remarkable find, Mr. Miller. Truly."

Norton sat back, thoughtful. "This is important," she said slowly. "Not just for you, Terry — for the county. For our history."

Terry nodded, excitement beginning to break through his shock. "People ought to know about it."

Whitmore agreed. "A discovery like this deserves to be documented."

Norton tapped her fingers lightly on the table, considering. "I think we should tell the newspaper. I could speak with Ted Bromfield at the Sentinel. He's fair, and he knows how to handle delicate stories."

Terry brightened. "I'd like that. I mean — if you think it's the right thing."

Whitmore gave a small nod. "I see no harm in it. And it may help preserve the context for future generations."

Norton smiled, satisfied. "Then I'll call him in the morning. We'll do this properly."

Whitmore gathered his gloves and slipped them back into his briefcase, then paused, thoughtful.

"There is one more thing," he said. "I'd like to show this drawing to a few colleagues — people who specialize in encoded imagery and nineteenth-century penwork. They may see something I've missed. Would you permit me to take it with me for a short time?"

Terry hesitated, glancing at the fragile sheet on the table. "Would a good copy do instead?"

Whitmore's face brightened. "Certainly. Do you have a copy?"

"Yes, I do," Terry said. He reached into his folder and withdrew Jake's careful reproduction, still crisp and clean. He handed it across the table.

Whitmore studied it, genuinely impressed. "Remarkable. Whoever made this copy did an excellent job. This will serve perfectly."

Terry felt a quiet swell of pride on Jake's behalf. "He worked hard on it, and he's only twelve."

"Amazing. I can see he's quite talented," Whitmore said, slipping the copy into a protective sleeve. "I'll return it to you when we meet on Saturday."

Bowling Night

Thursday after work, Terry Miller pulled his car into the angled parking spot outside *The Warren Sentinel* office. It was warm out and the front door was propped wide open. He stepped inside and immediately felt the rush of heat that had been generated by the printing presses. A couple of fans were running full blast.

"Afternoon, Terry," called Mrs. Dulaney from behind the counter. She was sorting bundles of the freshly printed weekly newspapers.

Terry had grown up with the *Sentinel.* Everybody in town read it — the church news, the socials, the Teen Scene, all the little things the *Northern Virginia Daily* never bothered with. If something made it into the Sentinel, folks noticed. It meant something.

"I'll take six copies," Terry said, trying — and failing — to keep the excitement out of his voice.

Mrs. Dulaney raised an eyebrow. "Six? My, my. Must be something worth reading."

Terry paid, gathered the stack under his arm, and stepped back out into the sunlight. He didn't make it to his car before he stopped, leaned against the fender, and opened the top paper.

There it was.

LOCAL MAN DISCOVERS LOST CIVIL WAR–ERA DRAWING

Historic Find Linked to Miss Alethea Marigold and Fallen Soldier Captain Charles Nation

And beneath the headline — the photograph.

Himself, holding the framed drawing, standing beside Mrs. Eleanor Norton, both of them looking solemn and proud under the library's porch light.

Terry felt a rush of heat in his chest, something like pride and disbelief tangled together. He read the article once, then again, slower this time, taking in every line — the mention of the four drawings, the confirmation of authenticity, the value, the history, the names of Charles and Alethea printed in black ink for the whole county to see.

By the time he folded the paper, he felt almost lightheaded. He had never been in the newspaper before. He had never been the center of anything before. And now — this.

He slid the six copies onto the passenger seat, sat behind the wheel, and let out a long breath that turned into a laugh. A real, full-bodied laugh of pure, unfiltered excitement.

"Wait till the guys at work see this," he said aloud.

He started the engine, still grinning, and pulled away from the curb.

That evening, right on schedule, Terry pulled into his father's driveway cut the engine and sat for a moment, looking at the folded newspaper on the passenger seat — his picture right there on the front page. He picked it up, smoothed the crease with his thumb, and felt that same warm rush he'd felt outside the Sentinel office.

"Pops is gonna be impressed," he murmured.

He grabbed a copy and headed to the porch. The light above the door flickered weakly, and he made a mental note to fix it.

Terence Miller answered the door with a distracted look, then immediately turned away, muttering about his cap. Terry stepped inside and held out the paper.

"Look, Pops. They put the story in this week's *Sentinel.* Front page."

His father took it, squinting at the headline, then at the photograph. "Well, I'll be," he said, a slow smile forming. "That's you, all right." But even as he said it, his gaze drifted toward the coat rack. "Now where's that cap… I know I left it right here."

Terry set the paper on the coffee table where his father would see it later. "It's fine, Pops. We'll find it after bowling."

But Terence was already shuffling toward the hallway, still talking about the cap.

Terry looked around the cluttered living room, the half-folded newspaper on the armchair, the glasses perched crookedly on the mantel where his father had forgotten them again. It hit him, as it had been hitting him more often lately, how old his dad looked. There had been a time — not that long ago in Terry's mind — when his father could bend a horseshoe in his bare hands and recite whole pages of the Sears catalog from memory just to impress his kids and their friends. Now he struggled to put on his shoes and was forever misplacing his glasses.

From down the hall came the sound of drawers opening and closing, then his father's voice, sharp with frustration. "I can't find my cap. I know I left it hanging on the hook by the door, but that cleaning woman hid it from me. She does it on purpose."

Terry knew that the cleaning woman was careful, almost overly gentle with his father. She straightened his papers, lined up his pill bottles, set his glasses in the same place every time. She loved his father. The idea that she would hide his cap on purpose made something twist in Terry's chest.

He walked toward the hallway. "Pops, you don't need your cap. It's warm out. Look at me — short sleeves, no cap."

"But I need my cap," his father insisted, dropping to one knee to peer under the sofa. "I always wear my cap when we go bowling."

From where he stood, Terry could see the thinness of his father's hair under the light of a lamp, the way his shoulders trembled as he shifted his weight. Getting down was hard enough; getting back up was another matter. Terry stepped in, slid an arm under his father's, and helped him struggle to his feet.

"Come on, Pops," he said quietly, helping his father to his feet. "The guys are waiting for us. We don't want to be late."

They moved toward the door together, Terry taking more of his father's weight than he let on. Bowling was already difficult for him — the steps, the ball, the balance. Terry knew it wouldn't be long before his father had to give it up, and with it would go the one regular thing that still tied them together.

Brother and sister, Cal and Rita, had their own lives now, out of town, busy with jobs and families. They called, they visited on holidays, but the day-to-day had fallen to Terry and stayed there. It had started back when his mother first got sick while he was still in high school. He hadn't gone off to college like Cal and Rita; it had felt wrong to leave. Then, after she died two years after he graduated, it seemed even more important to stay, to keep his father from coming apart altogether.

Once the two men were settled in the truck, the father tapped Terry on the shoulder and said, "I want to read that story in the paper when we get home. And we ought to mail copies to Cal and Rita. They'll want to read about what you found."

Terry felt his throat tighten, just a little. "Sure thing, Pops."

He backed out of the driveway, the evening sun barely catching the windshield, and headed toward the bowling alley — carrying with him the quiet hope that, for once, he'd given his father something to be proud of.

PART II

THE PAST AWAKENS

The Rumor

News of Terry Miller's discovery spread through Front Royal faster than wildfire.

By early the following morning, the whole town seemed to know — and to have an opinion about it. The unexpected result was a string of phone calls and encounters that left Terry feeling more bewildered than proud, as though the drawing he had treasured so dearly might not be a blessing after all.

The first call came at eight, from an insurance agent in town wanting to "have a friendly conversation" about protecting the document. The second came ten minutes later from an office in Winchester, the man on the line speaking with the smooth confidence of someone who had already decided what Terry ought to do was buy insurance to cover the drawing.

Then, just before he left for work, the phone rang again.

"Terry Miller," came the warm, rolling voice of Reverend Johnson. "I was delighted to see you in church Sunday and glad to see you in the paper this morning. A remarkable find. And should you ever decide to sell it, well… it would certainly be a kindness to remember the church in your giving."

At work that day, the guys were mostly curious about how he planned to spend all his "loot." Terry had to tell them—more than once—that he hadn't sold the picture and wasn't even sure he would. "I might end up donating it to a museum," he said, and left it at that.

By the time Terry pulled into the Safeway parking lot after work, he felt wrung out. He only needed bread, milk, and a few things for supper, but the moment he stepped inside the store he realized the whole town knew the story.

People smiled at him.

Nodded.
Stopped him in the aisles.

Even Bill Olinger, the store manager, came up, shook his hand, and congratulated him. "Great article!"

He was beginning to feel like a celebrity — and not in a way he enjoyed.

One woman told him that she had an old letter she'd like for him to look at to see if it was valuable.

Another woman touched his arm as he passed the produce bins.

"My son says there's a boy at school telling everyone he actually discovered that drawing first," she said, lowering her voice as though sharing a secret. She gave a sympathetic cluck. "I told him people will say anything once the newspaper gets involved."

Terry managed a polite smile, but inside something tightened.

A boy claiming he found it first?

He thanked her — Mrs. Hensley, he thought her name was — and moved on quickly, even turning his back at times so people wouldn't recognize him. He finished his shopping as fast as he could and headed out to the truck.

But once he'd loaded the groceries, he didn't start the engine. He sat there, staring out across the parking lot, the woman's words circling in his mind.

A boy at the school… claiming he found it first.

He needed to know who the boy was.

With a sigh, he climbed back out of the truck and went looking for the woman. He found her getting ready to check out.

"Ma'am?" he said gently. "About what you mentioned earlier — the boy at the school. Do you happen to know his name?"

She brightened. "Oh! No, I don't. My son just mentioned it in passing. Teenagers, you know how they are." She leaned in. "But I can ask him when he gets home. I'll give you a call."

"Yes, please give me a call. I'm in the book."

Terry thanked her and drove home, uneasy but grateful for the offer.

After dinner, he still had not received a call.

He waited.

The late afternoon stretched into evening. No call came.

Finally, as the sun dipped behind the ridge, he went to the kitchen drawer, pulled out the Front Royal phone book — barely a half-inch thick — and flipped through the H's. There she was: Hensley, Darlene.

He dialed.

"Oh, Terry! I'm so sorry," she said at once. "I meant to call you, but you know how it is — supper, laundry, everything happening at once." She covered the receiver and called out, "Tommy! What was the name of that boy you said was talking about the drawing?"

A muffled answer floated back. She returned to the line.

"He says it was Eddie Combs."

Terry felt something settle cold and heavy in his stomach. Eddie Combs.

"And Tommy says Eddie is telling everyone he's getting a reward."

The same boy Ray Shelley had mentioned — the one who'd nearly run over Ray's wife and boy outside the pawn shop.

The kid who'd rushed inside with the drawing. The kid who'd found it after Terry lost it.

Terry sat there holding the receiver, the pieces falling into place one by one.

He knew the name — just about everyone in town did. A boy with a hard home life, a father folks whispered about, a kid who drifted around the edges of things looking for trouble or maybe just looking for a place to belong.

I have to talk to that kid.

The next afternoon, Terry parked his truck along Happy Creek Road, just far enough from the Eastside Market that he wouldn't be obvious. The late-day sun slanted across the storefronts, throwing long shadows over the sidewalk. He'd seen Eddie around this stretch of town more than once — drifting near the market, cutting behind the houses, coasting along on that beat-up bicycle of his.

If the boy had a place where he felt safe, this was probably it.

Terry waited. Ten minutes. Fifteen.

Then he saw him.

Eddie came pedaling slowly up the road, his skinny frame hunched over the handlebars, the front wheel wobbling slightly. He hopped off near the market, let the bike clatter to the pavement, and went straight to the newspaper rack.

Terry took a breath, stepped out of the truck, and walked toward him.

"Eddie?" he said quietly.

The boy jerked, startled. He turned halfway, eyes narrowing, ready to bolt.

"What?" Eddie said, guarded.

"I'm Terry Miller."

"I know who you are."

Terry nodded. "I heard you might know something about the drawing."

"I didn't do anything wrong."

"I'm not saying you did," Terry said gently. "I just want to understand what happened."

Eddie scuffed the pavement with his shoe. "People talk too much."

"Sometimes they do," Terry agreed. "That's why I wanted to hear it from you."

"Why do you care?"

"I just want to get it right."

Eddie swallowed, eyes flicking away. "I gotta go."

He swung one leg over the bicycle frame.

Terry hesitated, then said, "Eddie… I'd like to talk with you about the reward."

The boy froze.

"There ain't no reward," he muttered, but the words wavered.

"I don't know about that," Terry said. "But if there is — or if people think there is — I need to hear your side. And I'd need to talk to your father too."

Eddie's face closed like a door slammed shut. "He don't care about any of this."

"Maybe," Terry said softly. "But it's still the right thing to do."

Eddie pushed off on the bike, the back wheel squeaking.

As he started to pedal away, Terry called after him, "I'd still like to talk, Eddie. Think about it."

The boy didn't look back.

"Give me a call," Terry added. "I'm in the book."

Eddie's pedaling hitched for half a second — just enough to show he'd heard — then he rode on, disappearing down Happy Creek Road, a thin figure swallowed by the lengthening shadows.

Terry stood there a moment longer, knowing this wasn't over.

Not by a long shot.

The Principal's Office

The front room of E. Wilson Morrison's office had the faint smell of chalk dust and mimeograph solution — the scent that clung to every school in America. Bill and Jeanie Sonnett sat side by side on the wooden bench along the wall, listening to the steady shuffle of children coming and going. Each child placed a folded attendance slip on the counter for the secretary, Mrs. Henshaw, who recorded the numbers with a practiced flick of her pencil.

The big wall clock ticked loudly in the quiet moments between footsteps.

The door swung open and in came Ed Stoup, the town's crossing guard, cap in hand.

"Mornin', Mrs. Henshaw," he said. "Had a little trouble at the corner by the drugstore. That new delivery truck keeps rolling through too fast. Nearly clipped the curb this time."

Mrs. Henshaw clucked her tongue. "I'll let Mr. Morrison know."

Ed nodded to Bill and Jeanie on his way out. "Sonnetts. Fine day."

Bill tipped his head. "Sure is."

A moment later, the door opened again and in stepped Mrs. Steed, Jake's homeroom teacher — trim skirt, sensible shoes, grade book tucked under her arm. She smiled warmly at the Sonnetts.

"Thank you for coming in. Mr. Morrison is ready for us."

They followed her into the principal's office, where E. Wilson Morrison rose from behind his desk. He was a tall man with a kind face, bald head, and thick glasses, the sort who could quiet a room just by standing in it.

"Bill, Jeanie — good to see you both. Please, sit. I'm sure you know Jake's teacher, Eula Steed."

They settled into the chairs across from him. Mrs. Steed took the one beside them, opening her grade book and laying out several sheets of paper.

"Well," she began, "I want to start by saying Jake is a good student. Truly. His work is solid across the board. His best subjects are math and art — an unusual combination, but not unheard of. He has a very orderly mind and a very creative one."

Jeanie smiled softly. "We've always seen that in him."

Mrs. Steed nodded. "Yes. And his handwriting is excellent, his arithmetic is neat, and his drawings…" She lifted one of the pages. "Well, you know."

Bill chuckled. "He gets that from his mother's side."

But Mrs. Steed's expression shifted slightly — not troubled, but thoughtful.

"There is one thing I wanted to mention," she said. "Jake is… a bit of a daydreamer. More than most boys his age. Just the other day I called his name twice before he heard me. He was staring off toward the window, completely gone to the world."

Jeanie's hands tightened in her lap. "I've noticed that at home too. Sometimes he doesn't answer right away. I thought it was just… childhood."

Before Mrs. Steed could respond, Morrison leaned back slightly, his expression softening with memory.

"You know," he said, "I saw Jake on the playground last fall. One of the younger boys — Tommy Whitaker — took a spill off the monkey bars. Scraped his knee pretty badly. Before any of the teachers even noticed, Jake was right there beside him, helping him up, talking to him real calm. Walked him all the way to the nurse's office like it was the most natural thing in the world."

He smiled at the Sonnetts. "That's the kind of boy he is. Steady. Kind. The sort who sees someone hurting and steps in."

Jeanie's eyes softened — but then she hesitated, folding her hands a little tighter.

"There is one other thing," she said quietly. "Lately, at breakfast, he's been complaining of headaches. Not every day, but enough that I've noticed."

Mrs. Steed and Morrison exchanged a brief, thoughtful glance — not alarmed, but attentive.

Morrison nodded slowly. "Thank you for mentioning that, Mrs. Sonnett. It may be nothing — children grow fast, and sometimes their bodies protest a bit. But paired with the daydreaming… it's something to keep an eye on."

Mrs. Steed added gently, "If it continues, it might be wise to have his doctor take a look. Just to rule out anything simple — vision, sinuses, even just needing more rest."

Bill reached over and touched Jeanie's hand. "We'll get it checked."

Mrs. Steed closed her grade book. "He truly is a pleasure to have in class."

Morrison stood, signaling the meeting's end. "Well," he said with a smile, "it seems we have a real Rembrandt here."

Bill grinned. "We think so. Thank you both for meeting with us."

Bill held the door for Jeanie as they stepped out of the school building, the late-morning sun bright on the gravel lot. They walked to the car in silence, each turning over the meeting in their own way. When Bill started the engine and pulled onto the road, he let out a long breath he'd been holding since they left Morrison's office.

"I didn't know about the headaches," he said quietly, eyes on the road.

Jeanie folded her hands in her lap. "They're not every day. But enough that I've noticed. He rubs his temples sometimes before he even starts eating."

Bill shook his head, jaw tightening with a father's worry. "I'm glad you mentioned it. I don't like the sound of that — headaches and drifting off like that in class."

"He's always been a thoughtful boy," Jeanie said, though her voice lacked its usual certainty.

"Thoughtful is one thing," Bill replied. "But this…if it's something physical, I don't want to wait around to see if there are more symptoms. No sense in letting something get ahead of us."

They passed the court house, the town hall and fire department, the familiar landmarks sliding by as Bill's thoughts churned.

"When he gets home from school this afternoon," Bill said firmly, "I want you to make an appointment with Dr. Sherman. Right away. No putting it off."

Jeanie nodded, relieved to have a clear course. "I will."

Bill's grip tightened on the wheel. "He's a good boy. A real good boy. And if something's bothering him — even a little — I want to know what it is."

The car rolled on toward home, the quiet between them no longer uncertain but purposeful, the kind that comes when two parents have made up their minds to look after their child with all the steadiness they can muster.

The Turning

Terry let himself into his small house just after six, the late-day light slanting across the living room floorboards. He loosened his tie, hung his jacket on the hook by the door, and stood for a moment in the quiet. His thoughts drifted — as they had all day — to Eddie.

Had he handled that conversation right? Had he pushed too hard? Or not enough?

He replayed the boy's guarded expression, the way Eddie had hovered between wanting help and wanting to bolt. Terry rubbed the back of his neck. Maybe the kid would never call. Maybe he'd scared him off.

He had just sat down with the evening paper when the phone rang — sharp, urgent, slicing through the quiet.

Terry snatched it up. "Hello?"

A shaky voice on the other end: "Mr. Miller… please… help me!"

"Eddie? Eddie, where are you?"

"At the pay phone by the grocery store… I'll be in back… please hurry…"

That was all Terry needed. He grabbed his keys and was out the door before the receiver settled back into its cradle.

The area behind the grocery store was where the trash cans were kept, lit only by the glow from the back door and a pale streetlamp. Eddie stood there hunched against the wall, arms wrapped around himself. When he lifted his face, Terry's breath caught.

A black eye already swelling shut. A bloody nose. A split, swollen lip.

"Lord, Eddie…" Terry moved toward him carefully, not wanting to startle him. "What happened?"

"The old man beat me up," Eddie whispered. "'Cause his new girlfriend was nice to me. I ran away. I'm scared."

Terry put a steady hand on his shoulder. "You're safe now. Come on—we're going to the hospital."

Eddie didn't argue. He just nodded, trembling.

***

Warren Memorial Hospital — Emergency Room

The nurses took one look at Eddie and ushered him straight back. Terry wasn't allowed to follow, so he sat in the waiting room, hands clasped, foot tapping a restless rhythm on the linoleum floor. The clock on the wall ticked too loudly. A vending machine with a flickering light hummed in the corner. Every time a door opened, Terry looked up.

Finally, the doctor emerged with a police officer — the night-duty deputy, uniform crisp, hat tucked under his arm.

The doctor spoke first. "Mr. Miller? The boy's going to be all right. He's bruised up, but nothing broken. We've cleaned him up."

Terry nodded, relief loosening his shoulders.

The deputy stepped forward. "He told us his father hit him. Says it's happened before."

Terry's jaw tightened. "He can't go back there."

"That's what he said too," the deputy replied. "He's scared to death of the man."

The doctor added, “He asked if you were still here.”

“I’m not going anywhere,” Terry said.

A nurse appeared. “He can see you now.”

Eddie sat on the edge of the bed, blanket around his shoulders, his face cleaned but still swollen and bruised. When Terry stepped inside, the boy’s eyes lifted immediately, full of relief and exhaustion.

“Mr. Miller…” Eddie’s voice was thin, shaky. “I’m glad you’re still here.”

“I told you I wasn’t going anywhere,” Terry said, pulling the chair close.

Eddie swallowed hard, then glanced toward the door where the deputy had just stepped out to speak with the doctor.

“I’m glad he’s gonna talk to my father,” Eddie whispered. “But… it won’t matter. He don’t want me around anyway.”

Terry leaned in, gentle but steady. “What do you mean?”

Eddie’s eyes filled, but he blinked fast, trying to hold it together.

“He accused me of messing with his woman,” he said, voice cracking. “Said I was trying to steal her from him. I wasn’t. I swear I wasn’t. She just… she was nice to me. That’s all.”

“I know, Eddie,” Terry said quietly. “I know.”

Eddie wiped his nose with the back of his hand. “He got real mad. Said I was trouble. Said I was trying to make him look bad. Then he hit me and kicked me out. Told me not to come back.”

Terry felt something tighten in his chest — anger, sorrow, and a fierce protectiveness he hadn’t expected.

"You listen to me," he said, keeping his voice calm. "None of that is your fault. Not one bit. A grown man ought to know better."

Eddie looked down at his hands. "I didn't know where else to go. I didn't want to bother you, but… I didn't have nobody."

"You did the right thing calling me," Terry said. "You hear me? The right thing."

A soft knock sounded, and the deputy stepped back into the room. He looked at Eddie first, then at Terry.

"I've spoken with your father," the deputy said. "He made it clear he doesn't want you home tonight. Or anytime soon, far as I can tell."

Eddie's shoulders sagged, but there was no surprise in his face — only a tired acceptance.

The deputy continued, "So here's what we're gonna do. Mr. Miller, if you're willing, the boy can stay with you for a while. I'll make sure his father keeps his distance. And if he so much as thinks about causing trouble, he'll answer to me."

Terry nodded without hesitation. "He'll stay with me."

Eddie looked up, eyes shining with something like hope — fragile, but real.

"Thank you," he whispered.

Terry rested a hand on his shoulder. "You're safe now. We'll figure the rest out together."

They left the hospital.

When they arrived at Terry's house, he unlocked the front door and stepped aside so Eddie could enter first. The boy hesitated on the threshold, shoulders hunched, eyes darting around the small living room as if expecting someone to jump out at him. He clutched the paper bag of ointment and bandages the nurse had given him.

"It ain't much," Terry said gently, "but it's warm, and it's quiet."

Eddie nodded without looking up. "It's fine."

He stood there stiffly, not sure where to go or what to do with himself. Terry could feel the awkwardness hanging in the air — the kind that comes when a boy has never been welcomed anywhere and doesn't know how to act when someone finally tries.

"You can sit," Terry said, motioning to the sofa.

Eddie perched on the edge of it like he expected to be told to move any second.

Terry went into the kitchen. "You hungry?"

"No," Eddie muttered.

Terry paused. "You sure?"

A pause.

Then, quietly: "Yeah. I mean… maybe."

Terry warmed up some leftover stew and brought it out with a slice of bread. Eddie stared at it for a moment, then grabbed the spoon and began shoveling it in with a speed that startled Terry. Every bite made him wince — his split lip pulling — but he didn't slow down.

"Easy," Terry said softly. "It's not going anywhere."

Eddie didn't answer. He just kept eating until the bowl was empty, then wiped his mouth with the back of his hand.

When he finally looked up, some of the shyness had burned off, replaced by a flash of anger — hot, defensive, the kind that had kept him alive in a house where kindness was a foreign language.

"When I get bigger," Eddie said suddenly, voice tight, "I'm gonna go back there and teach that son of a bitch who's the tough guy."

Terry sat down across from him, not flinching at the language or the fury behind it.

"I get why you feel that way," he said. "Anybody would. But listen to me, Eddie — you don't owe that man a thing. Not a fight, not a word, not a look back over your shoulder."

Eddie's jaw clenched. "He deserves it."

"Maybe he does," Terry said. "But you don't deserve the trouble it'd bring you."

Eddie looked away, breathing hard through his nose. The anger wasn't gone, but it had softened around the edges, replaced by something more fragile — hurt, confusion, the ache of being thrown away by the only parent he had.

Terry stood. "Come on. I'll show you where you can sleep."

He led Eddie down the short hallway to the spare room — really just a storage room with a narrow bed, a dresser, and a lamp. Terry pulled fresh sheets and pillow case from the hall closet and tossed them in on the bed.

Eddie stepped inside slowly, as if afraid the room might vanish if he blinked.

"You can put your things in the dresser," Terry said. "Bathroom's right across the hall. My bedroom's at the end. If you need anything, just knock."

Eddie nodded, still not speaking.

Terry started to leave, then paused in the doorway. "You're safe here, Eddie. That's not gonna change tonight."

For a long moment, Eddie didn't move. Then he whispered, barely audible:

"Thanks."

"Try to get to sleep. In the morning, we'll have a big breakfast, and I'll drive you to school."

Terry gave a small nod and closed the door halfway — not all the way, not enough to make the boy feel shut in.

As he walked back down the hall, Terry felt the weight of the day settle on him — the fear in Eddie's voice on the phone, the bruises, the anger, the trust the boy had placed in him without even knowing how to ask for it.

It was going to be an adjustment for both of them. Awkward. Messy. Maybe hard.

But Terry knew one thing with absolute clarity:

He wasn't letting that boy face the world alone again.

The Doctor's Office

Dr. Elizabeth Sherman's office sat on Virginia Avenue, a one-story yellow-brick building just a block and a half from the Sonnetts' house.

Rather than entering through the main door into the waiting room, Joanie Sonnett and Jake stepped into her office using the side door directly to the receptionist's desk. The place smelled faintly of antiseptic and lemon polish — the same smell Jake remembered from every visit since he was a baby.

Behind the desk sat Mrs. Eva Thomas, her white hair swept back in a way that made her resemble George Washington in profile. Emmett had pointed it out once, and now Jake could never unsee it.

Mrs. Thomas peered over her glasses. "Well, good morning, Mrs. Sonnett. And Jake. You're getting too tall for this place."

Jake managed a small smile.

"Dr. Sherman will be with you shortly," she said, sliding a clipboard toward Joanie. "Just sign in and have a seat."

Joanie thanked her and guided Jake to the waiting room — a row of wooden chairs, a low table with dog-eared *Highlights* magazines, and a fish tank bubbling quietly in the corner. Jake watched a single orange fish drift behind a plastic castle, its movements slow and hypnotic.

He felt his mother's eyes on him. "You doing all right?"

"Yeah," he said, though he wasn't sure.

Before long, Mrs. Thomas called, "Jake Sonnett?"

Jake and his mother followed her down the hallway to the exam room. A moment later, the door opened and Dr. Elizabeth Sherman stepped in.

She was short — barely five feet — with dark hair pulled back into a tight bun. Her white coat was crisp, her expression brisk but not unkind, and she had a friendly face with dark, intelligent eyes that told you right away there was a sharp mind working behind them. Jake had always thought she was the best doctor in the entire world.

"Good morning, Jake," she said, consulting his chart. "My, you've grown. I'm going to have to raise my height bar again."

Jake smiled faintly.

Dr. Sherman was the first woman doctor in Warren County — a fact she never mentioned, but everyone in town did. She wore her wristwatch with the face on the inside of her wrist, something Jake had noticed years ago and still found curious.

"So," she said, pulling up her stool, "your mother tells me you've been having some headaches. And a few spells where you're not quite aware of things around you."

Jake nodded. "Sometimes I just… drift off. I don't mean to."

"Hmm." She tapped her pen lightly against the chart. "Let's take a look."

She examined his eyes with a small light, checked his reflexes, listened to his heart and lungs. Then she had him stand on one foot, then the other. Walk heel-to-toe across the room. Touch his finger to his nose with his eyes closed.

Jake did everything she asked, though he felt a little silly.

Dr. Sherman watched him closely, her brow furrowed in concentration. When he finished, she sat back on her stool and folded her hands.

"Well," she said, "I don't see anything obvious. His reflexes are normal, balance is good, vision is unchanged. Nothing here gives me a clear diagnosis."

Joanie's face tightened. "Then what's causing it?"

Dr. Sherman shook her head gently. "I can't say for certain. And I don't want to guess. What I *do* want is for Jake to see a neurologist — someone who specializes in these things."

"A neurologist?" Joanie repeated, her voice thin.

"Yes. There's an excellent one at the University of Virginia Hospital in Charlottesville. I'll write a referral. They have equipment and tests I don't have here."

Jake looked at his mother. Her hands were clasped tightly in her lap.

"Is it serious?" Joanie asked.

Dr. Sherman's tone softened. "I'm not saying that. I'm saying I want to be thorough. Jake is a bright boy, and these episodes — the drifting, the headaches — they deserve a closer look. Better to rule things out than to let them linger."

Joanie nodded slowly. "All right. If you think it's best."

"I do," Dr. Sherman said. "And I'll call ahead so they know to expect you."

She placed a reassuring hand on Joanie's arm. "You're doing the right thing."

As they left the office, Jake glanced back at Dr. Sherman. She was already writing notes, her watch face glinting from the inside of her wrist.

Joanie squeezed his shoulder as they stepped into the sunlight.

"I don't like it," she said quietly. "But I'm glad someone else will take a look."

Jake didn't know what to say. He only knew that the fish tank, the waiting room, and Dr. Sherman's steady voice all felt very far away now — as if he were drifting again, only this time with his eyes wide open.

Clara Whitlow was already standing on her porch when Jeanie and Jake pulled into the driveway. She had Emmett beside her, holding a half-eaten oatmeal cookie and looking perfectly content. Clara waved them over with the urgency of someone who had been waiting all morning for news.

"Jeanie! How'd it go? Come on, tell me everything."

Jeanie managed a tired smile. "Thank you for watching Emmett. I don't know what I'd do without you."

"Oh, nonsense," Clara said, brushing it off. "Now what did Dr. Sherman say? That woman could diagnose a flea at fifty paces."

Jeanie took Emmett's hand and guided him toward the house. "She examined Jake. Eyes, balance, reflexes… all of it. She didn't find anything wrong."

Clara followed, leaning in as if the details might slip away if she didn't catch them fast enough. "Well, that's good, isn't it?"

"Yes," Jeanie said, though her voice wavered. "But she wants him to see a neurologist in Charlottesville. Just to be sure."

Clara's eyebrows shot up. "A neurologist? Lord have mercy."

Jeanie stiffened. "She said it's just precaution."

Clara lowered her voice, glancing around though no one else was in earshot. "You know… I have a cousin down in Roanoke. Had the same exact thing."

Jeanie froze. "The same… what do you mean?"

"Oh, the drifting off. The staring spells. Headaches in the morning." Clara nodded with the certainty of someone who loved a good medical comparison. "Turned out to be a form of epilepsy. Mild, they said, but still epilepsy."

Jeanie felt her stomach drop. "Epilepsy?"

"Yes, but don't you worry," Clara said, patting her arm in a way that did nothing to help. "He's fine now. Mostly. Just has to be careful. And take medicine. And avoid certain things. But he's fine."

Jeanie swallowed hard, her throat suddenly dry. "Dr. Sherman didn't say anything about that."

"Well, she wouldn't," Clara said. "Doctors never tell you the worst until they're sure. But I'm telling you — it sounds just like my cousin."

Jake, who had been lingering by the porch steps, looked up sharply. "Mama…?"

Jeanie forced a smile, though her heart was pounding. "It's all right, sweetheart. Let's get inside."

Clara kept talking, oblivious to the rising panic in Jeanie's eyes. "I'm just saying — better to be prepared. These things can sneak up on you."

"Thank you, Clara," Jeanie said, a little too quickly. "I appreciate you watching Emmett."

Clara nodded, satisfied she had been helpful. "Anytime, dear. You let me know what that specialist says."

When Clara finally headed back across the yard, Jeanie stood on the porch for a long moment, one hand pressed to her chest. The morning sun felt too bright, the air too thin.

Epilepsy. The word echoed in her mind like a bell tolling.

She took a steadying breath, gathered her boys, and ushered them inside — doing her best to keep her voice calm, even as her worry deepened into something colder and sharper than before.

The Marigold Mansion

The drizzle had settled into a steady mist by the time Terry's truck rattled up the long, rutted drive. Eddie leaned forward in the passenger seat, peering through the windshield.

"Is this it?" he asked.

"This is it," Terry said.

The Marigold Mansion rose out of the fog like a memory that had been left out in the weather too long. The house was built of heavy, dark stone, the kind that held the cold even in summer, and its steep gables and tall chimneys loomed through the mist like the ribs of some ancient creature. Once, the place had been grand—an ornate villa with a deep wraparound porch and carved brackets under the eaves.

You could still see the bones of that ambition in the rooflines and the tall, narrow windows. But time had stripped away the finery. The porch was nearly gone now, little more than a sagging platform of rotted boards. The decorative woodwork had fallen away in pieces, leaving only ghost-shapes where it had once clung.

Grass and weeds stood knee-high across the property, slick with rain. Ivy had begun to climb the stone walls, probing into cracks, and a young sapling had forced its way up through what remained of the front steps, splitting the boards as if the house itself were coming apart at the seams.

Every ground-floor window was boarded over with gray, weather-beaten planks, some warped, some nailed on crookedly, as though the house had been shuttered in a hurry and then forgotten.

Terry cut the engine. "Whitmore should be along in a few minutes. Thought we'd look around a bit."

They stepped out into the cool air. Eddie shoved his hands into the pockets of the jacket that was much too big for him and followed Terry up the overgrown path. The wet grass slapped against their legs.

"Creepy," Eddie muttered, though there was fascination in his voice.

"Old places get that way," Terry said.

He led Eddie around the side of the house, scanning the property. "Whitmore mentioned there's a family plot somewhere back here. Small one. I'd like to find it."

But the weeds were too thick, the brambles too tangled. Everything beyond a few feet was swallowed in green.

"Can't see a thing," Terry said. "We'll have to come back when it's not raining."

Eddie kicked at a clump of weeds. "Bet it's all covered up. Like the house is trying to hide it."

Terry gave him a sideways look. "That's a pretty sharp observation."

Eddie shrugged, embarrassed.

A car engine approached from the road. Moments later, a dark sedan pulled up behind Terry's truck. Professor Whitmore stepped out, adjusting his hat against the drizzle.

"Morning, Terry!" he called. Then he noticed Eddie. "Oh—hello there. Didn't realize you had company."

Terry placed a steady hand on Eddie's shoulder. "This is Eddie. He's been staying with me for a bit. Thought he might enjoy seeing the place."

Whitmore blinked, surprised but not displeased. "Well, Eddie, good to meet you. Always glad to have another pair of eyes. Old houses like this reward careful looking."

Eddie nodded shyly.

Whitmore gestured toward the porch. "Shall we?"

They followed him up the sagging steps. Whitmore tested each board with the toe of his shoe. "Careful here. This porch was spectacular once—columns, railings, the whole bit. Now it's more hole than porch."

He produced a heavy brass key from his coat pocket. "The heirs—distant cousins out in California—gave me access. They're selling off anything of value and donating the rest. I'm here on a grant to document as much as I can before it all disappears."

He tapped the folded papers in his hand. "I've got a list I'm working from. Furniture, documents, architectural details, anything that tells the story."

The key turned with a reluctant groan. The door swung inward, releasing a breath of cool, stale air.

Inside, it was surprisingly dark. The only light peeking through the spaces between the boards on the windows.

The house felt like a museum abandoned mid-sentence. Each room they passed had a fireplace—some with cracked tiles, others with mantels still intact. A few pieces of furniture remained: a chair with one leg missing, a sideboard with peeling parquet, a sofa draped in a dusty sheet.

Eddie moved slowly, taking everything in. "Bet this place was real fancy once."

"It was," Whitmore said. "At one time there were hundreds of books here. A private library that would've made a scholar weep."

"What happened to them?" Terry asked.

"Sold," Whitmore said simply. "Most of them. A few donated. A few lost."

Terry frowned. "Seems like a shame."

Whitmore gave him an approving look. "It is."

They climbed the wide staircase, their footsteps echoing in the empty house. At the top, there was more light. Whitmore paused.

"Would you like to see Alethea's bedroom?"

Terry nodded, and Whitmore led them down the hall to a room at the end. The door creaked open to reveal a large chamber with a four-poster bed still standing, its carved posts rising toward the ceiling, the coverlet coated in dust.

On the mantel above the fireplace sat an old clock—tall, elegant, its lower glass panel painted with a pastoral scene.

Terry stepped toward it, drawn in. "That's beautiful."

"Early nineteenth century," Whitmore said. "A fine piece. It's on my list."

Terry leaned closer to the clock, studying it with the quiet reverence of someone who understood what he was touching.

The lower glass panel held a reverse painting — bright, crisp, and untouched by time, the colors protected on the inside of the glass. A house, a tree, a rising sun: the scene looked as if it had been waiting decades for someone to open the door again. At the very center of the sun, where the painter had left a small circle of clear glass for the once polished brass pendulum bob to show through.

Terry crouched to study the painted glass. "Mind if I open the door?"

"Just be careful," Whitmore said.

Terry found the small keyhole on the side, turned the tiny brass key, and swung the door open. Inside, the pendulum weights hung motionless, and the special crank rested in its slot—one for winding the time, the other for the chime.

Inside the case, two heavy lead weights hung motionless.

Terry glanced back at Whitmore. "Mind if I wind it?"

Whitmore hovered behind him, uneasy. "I'm not sure winding it is a good idea. These old movements can be temperamental."

Terry shook his head gently. "This one's weight-driven. As long as the cords are sound, she'll be fine."

Whitmore hesitated. "Still…"

"I know what I'm doing," Terry said, calm and certain. "I'll take responsibility."

He lifted the small crank from its resting place and fitted it onto the left-hand winding arbor on the dial.

"This arbor raises the time weight," he said quietly.

He turned the crank slowly while gently lifting the weight with his other hand. The weight rose inch by inch, the ratchet giving a soft, dry click with each turn.

When the weight reached a comfortable height, Terry moved the crank to the right-hand arbor.

"And this one lifts the strike weight."

He wound in the opposite direction, careful and deliberate. Another series of clicks, another slow rise of a lead weight.

Whitmore leaned in despite himself. Eddie watched from a few steps back, eyes wide.

Terry replaced the crank inside the case, then reached for the pendulum. He gave it a gentle push.

For a breath, nothing happened.

Then the clock answered with a single, soft **tick**.

Another **tick**. Then **tock**.

The pendulum settled into a smooth, confident arc, swinging behind the label as if it had never stopped. The sound filled the dusty bedroom — steady, measured, alive.

Eddie's voice was barely above a whisper. "It sounds like a heartbeat."

Whitmore exhaled, tension easing from his shoulders. "Well… I'll be damned. She still runs."

Terry watched the pendulum for a long moment, the rhythm settling into the room like a pulse returning to a long-forgotten body.

"Some things," he said quietly, "just need someone to start them again." He closed the clock door and locked it.

The clock ticked steadily now, the pendulum swinging with a confidence it hadn't known in decades. Terry stepped back just enough to watch the dial. Whitmore hovered near the door, arms folded, still half-expecting something to go wrong. Eddie stood at the foot of the bed, eyes fixed on the clock face.

A faint shift inside the case — a soft click, the gathering pallet lifting the hammer.

Terry murmured, "She's about to strike."

Whitmore blinked. "Already?"

"The clock hands say it's three o'clock," Eddie observed. "Wrong time."

There was a tiny pause, like the clock drawing breath.

Then—

DING.

A bright, ringing note — sharp, metallic, clean. Not a gong, not a bell tower, but the crisp strike of a small hammer on a brass bell. The sound cut through the dusty stillness of the room with startling clarity.

A heartbeat later:

DING.

Whitmore let out a slow breath, the tension easing from his shoulders.

And then the third:

DING.

The final chime hung in the air, vibrating faintly in the wooden mantel and the bedposts, as if the house itself were listening.

Eddie whispered, "It sounds like it's waking up."

Terry nodded, eyes on the pendulum. "That's how these clocks are. They don't roar back to life. They announce themselves."

Whitmore shook his head in quiet amazement. "I never thought I'd hear that clock strike again."

The last chime faded into the stillness of the room, leaving only the steady **tick-tick-tick** of the pendulum. Terry stood close to the clock, his expression softening. Almost without thinking, he ran his hands along the sides of the case — a quiet, affectionate gesture, as if telling the old thing, *Good job. You're still with us.*

Whitmore watched him with a mixture of relief and lingering nerves. "Well… I suppose she's sturdier than she looks."

Terry didn't answer. His fingertips had drifted down the carved columns, tracing the grooves worn smooth by time. Then he slipped one hand beneath the base, feeling along the underside where the scroll feet met the lower molding.

His brow furrowed.

"What's this?" he murmured.

Whitmore straightened. "What's what?"

"There's… a lever." Terry's voice held a puzzled note. "Right here. Built into the bottom rail."

Eddie stepped closer, eyes wide. "A secret one?"

Terry didn't speculate. He simply tested it with his thumb.

The lever moved.

There was a soft internal click — not loud, but unmistakably mechanical — followed by a small, hollow shift inside the case. Then, from the underside of the clock, a narrow compartment dropped open with a muted wooden thump, like a drawer that had been waiting decades for someone to remember it existed.

Something fell into Terry's hand.

A small, worn, hand-stitched, leather-bound book.

The leather was cracked with age, the edges softened by handling. No title on the cover. No clasp. Just a simple, time-darkened volume, small enough to fit inside the palm of Terry's hand.

Whitmore's breath caught. "Good Lord… I had no idea there was a hidden compartment in that piece."

Eddie stared at the book as if it might start glowing. "What is it?"

Terry turned it over gently, the way one handles something fragile and important. "It's a book of some kind."

"I'm almost afraid to open it," he said, his voice low. "I think you should do the honors."

He held the book out to Whitmore.

For a heartbeat, Whitmore didn't move. His eyes flicked from Terry's face to the book, then back again — as if confirming that Terry truly meant it. Then he reached out and took the small volume with both hands, the way a person receives something fragile, or sacred.

He opened it carefully, easing the front cover back so the old leather wouldn't protest.

Terry and Eddie leaned in a little to see what the book revealed.

The pages were filled from top to bottom with neat handwriting. Every line was steady, every letter shaped with care. But the words themselves were illegible.

Whitmore turned a few pages, then a few more, his brow drawing in as he studied the script. He wasn't hurried about it. He took his time, the way a man does when he knows the past won't be rushed.

"Well," he said at last, "this is interesting."

Terry waited, hands in his pockets, letting Whitmore work it through.

"I'm fairly good at recognizing European languages," Whitmore went on. "Comes with the territory. Latin roots, the Germanic families, the Romance branches… even the more obscure ones."

He flipped back to the first page and looked again, as if a second glance might coax meaning from the lines.

"These letters are Indo-European in shape," he said. "Nothing unusual about the alphabet itself."

Eddie edged closer. "So what's it say?"

Whitmore shook his head. "I can't tell you. Because this—" he tapped the page lightly with one finger "—isn't any language I know."

Terry looked at him. "Then who can read it?"

Whitmore closed the book halfway, not shutting it, just holding it in his palms. "My best guess is, it's a code. Either a simple substitution code or else someone took the time to invent a system of their own."

Eddie's eyes widened. "Like a secret diary?"

"Could be."

Whitmore turned a few more pages, his thumb resting lightly against the edge of the paper. The writing was neat, careful, and consistent from one page to the next. He studied it without rushing, the way a man does who's spent his life reading the past.

"It's not unusual," he said after a moment. "People used to write in code more often than you'd think."

Terry looked over his shoulder. "They did?"

"Oh yes." Whitmore nodded, still scanning the lines. "Beatrix Potter — the woman who wrote *Peter Rabbit* — kept an entire diary in code. No one could read it for years. And Samuel Pepys, the English diarist, did the same thing. Wrote his private thoughts in a shorthand only he understood."

Eddie's eyes widened. "So folks really did that? Just… made up their own way of writing?"

"Quite a few did," Whitmore said. "Especially if they had something they didn't want others to see."

He closed the book halfway, not snapping it shut, just holding it in his hands as if weighing what it meant.

"So this isn't strange at all," he went on. "Whoever wrote this had a reason. And they took the trouble to hide it well."

Whitmore held the little book a moment longer, then closed it gently and slipped it into the inside pocket of his coat.

"I'll take this back to my office," he said. "Give it a careful look. No promises, but I might be able to make sense of the pattern, if there is one. Also, if it is indeed written in a code, I'll check with my colleagues to see if anyone will tackle decoding it."

Terry nodded. "Please let me know what you find."

Eddie was still staring at the clock, listening to its steady ticking. "Feels like we woke the whole house up," he said.

Whitmore smiled at that. "Maybe you did."

They made their way downstairs, stepping carefully on the loose boards.

Whitmore locked up.

Outside, the drizzle had eased to a mist.

Whitmore paused beside his car. "Thank you both for coming up today. I wasn't expecting a discovery like that."

"Neither were we," Terry said.

Eddie gave a small wave.

"Goodbye, Eddie. Take care of yourself."

Whitmore climbed into his car and started the engine. He gave them a last nod before easing down the long, overgrown drive.

Terry and Eddie stood for a moment, watching the car disappear into the gray.

"Well," Terry said, "that was something."

Eddie looked back at the house, its boarded windows and sagging porch softened by the mist. "Do you think there's more stuff hidden in there?"

"There might be," Terry said. "Old places hold on to things."

They headed for the truck. Terry started the engine, and the heater hummed to life. As they pulled away, the mansion faded back into the trees, the steady ticking of the clock still echoing faintly in their minds.

Charlottesville

They hadn't even cleared the Front Royal town limits before the questions began.

"Where are we going?" Jake Sonnett asked from the back seat of the car, pulling his jacket tighter around him. "Why'd we have to get up so early? I'm gonna miss my Saturday morning shows."

Jake's father gripped the steering wheel with both hands and kept his eyes on the wet road ahead. "We're going to see a doctor, son. The one Dr. Sherman recommended."

Jake frowned. "But I feel fine."

"I know you do," his mother seated in the front passenger seat said softly. "This doctor just wants to take a look. Make sure everything's all right."

Jake slumped back against the seat, unsatisfied. "Is it far?"

"Not too far," Bill said. "Charlottesville."

Jake made a small sound — half sigh, half protest — and looked down at the drawing pad resting on his lap. He traced the edge of the cardboard cover with his thumb, restless, uncertain.

"Do I have to get a shot?" he asked.

"Probably not," Jeanie said. "This doctor mostly talks and listens."

"And looks," Bill added. "He's just gonna check you over."

Jake stared out the window at the blurred shapes of trees sliding past in the drizzle. "I don't like doctors."

"I know," Jeanie said, having twisted around so she faced her son. "But this one's supposed to be very nice."

Jake was quiet for a moment, then said, "Why today? It's Saturday."

Bill and Jeanie exchanged a quick glance — the kind that carried a whole conversation in a heartbeat.

"Because he had an opening," Bill said. "And we didn't want to wait."

Jake nodded, though his brow stayed furrowed. "I'm still gonna miss the really good shows."

Jeanie smiled faintly. "You can catch them next week."

Jake wasn't convinced, but he let it go. He shifted the drawing pad again, holding it like something that might steady him.

The rain had settled into a thin, steady drizzle, the kind that blurred the edges of the world without ever quite committing to a storm.

The sky hung low and gray over the Valley, the Blue Ridge softened into a single long shadow. Bill kept both hands on the wheel, leaning forward slightly as if that might help him see farther down the wet ribbon of Route 340.

Jeanie leaned over the back of the front seat and smoothed Jake's hair, though it didn't need smoothing. "Don't worry, dear. Everything's going to be all right."

Jake forced a smile.

"You know," Bill said, pitching his voice toward cheerfulness, "your mother tells me you're working on something for an art contest at school."

Jake hesitated. "I'm thinking about it."

"Well, I think you ought to," Bill said. "You've got a good eye. Always have."

Jeanie added, "Mrs. Steed says you're the best drawer in the whole sixth grade."

Jake looked down, embarrassed but pleased. "I'm not the best."

"You're pretty close," Bill said, glancing over with a half-smile.

They were trying — both of them — to keep the air light, to keep the drive from feeling like what it was: a long road toward an answer none of them wanted to name. But beneath their words ran a quiet current of fear, steady as the rain tapping against the windshield.

Jeanie watched the wipers sweep back and forth, back and forth, the rhythm almost hypnotic. She kept seeing Jake at the breakfast table, staring past her with that faraway look, the spoon slipping from his hand. She kept hearing Clara's voice — *my cousin had the same thing, turned out to be epilepsy* — and no matter how she tried to push it aside, the thought clung to her like damp wool.

Bill cleared his throat. "Dr. Franklin comes highly recommended. Folks say he's patient. Thorough."

Jeanie nodded, though her hands were tight in her lap. "That's what we want."

Jake looked from one parent to the other. "Am I… am I in trouble?"

"Oh, honey," Jeanie said, turning toward him. "No. Not at all. We just want to make sure everything's all right. That's all."

Bill added, “Think of it like a check-up. Just a longer one.”

Jake nodded again, but his shoulders stayed small and drawn in.

They drove on in silence for a while, the road winding gently through the foothills. The rain softened to mist, then thickened again, as if the weather couldn’t make up its mind.

When they reached Charlottesville, the hospital rose ahead of them — a tall, pale building with long windows and a sense of quiet purpose. Bill pulled into the parking lot and cut the engine. For a moment, none of them moved.

“All right,” he said softly. “Let’s go meet the doctor.”

The neurology department waiting room smelled faintly of floor polish and something medicinal. A nurse in a crisp white uniform led them down a hallway lined with framed photographs of the hospital’s early days — horse-drawn ambulances, stern-faced doctors in stiff collars.

Dr. Harold Franklin met them at the door to his office.

He was taller than Bill expected, with dark hair combed neatly back, a slight thinning at the crown, and thick eyebrows that gave his face a look of thoughtful gravity. His voice, when he spoke, carried that soft-r Virginia cadence — warm, steady, unhurried.

“Mr. and Mrs. Sonnett,” he said, shaking their hands. “And this must be Jake.”

Jake managed a small “Yes, sir.”

Dr. Franklin smiled gently. “I’m glad you’re here. Why don’t we talk for a few minutes, and then we’ll get started.”

He invited Bill and Jeanie to sit in two chairs near his desk while Jake waited just outside with the nurse, who handed him a small stack of picture books.

When the door closed, Dr. Franklin folded his hands on the desk.

"Now," he said, "I've read Dr. Sherman's notes. She describes episodes where Jake seems unaware of his surroundings, along with headaches. I'd like to run a series of tests today to help us understand what's going on."

Jeanie leaned forward. "Doctor… my neighbor said these spells might be epilepsy. Is that… is that possible?"

Dr. Franklin nodded slowly, not dismissing her fear, not feeding it either. "It's one possibility. There are several types of seizures, some very mild. But there are also other explanations — migraines, fainting spells, even simple lapses of attention. Today's tests will help us sort through those."

Bill asked, "What kind of tests?"

Dr. Franklin opened a folder and spoke with the calm precision of someone who had explained this many times, but never carelessly.

"First, we'll do an electroencephalogram — an EEG."

He paused to let the words settle.

"That's a test that measures the electrical activity of the brain. We place small electrodes on the scalp — they don't hurt — and record the brain's patterns. Certain kinds of seizures leave characteristic traces."

Jeanie swallowed. "Will he be awake?"

"Yes," Dr. Franklin said. "Awake, and very still. It takes about an hour."

"Next, we'll do a pneumoencephalogram."

He said it gently, knowing the word itself could frighten.

"That's an imaging test we use to look at the brain's structure. It helps us see if there's any pressure, swelling, or abnormality that might explain his symptoms."

Jeanie's hands tightened. "Is it… painful?"

"There may be some discomfort," he said honestly. "We remove a small amount of spinal fluid and replace it with air so the brain's outline shows clearly on X-ray. Jake will be given something to help him relax. We'll take good care of him."

Bill nodded, jaw set.

"We'll also run a neurological examination."

"Reflexes, balance, coordination, eye movements — all the things that help us understand how the nervous system is functioning."

He closed the folder gently.

"All told, the tests will take about three hours. You're welcome to stay in the waiting room, but most parents find it easier to step out for a bit. There's a Howard Johnson's just down the road. You can get some lunch, some coffee."

Jeanie's voice was small. "Will you… will you come get us if anything is wrong?"

Dr. Franklin's expression softened. "Mrs. Sonnett, if I learn anything concerning, you'll be the first to know. But right now, we're gathering information. That's all."

She nodded, though her eyes shone.

Bill stood and offered his hand. "Thank you, Doctor."

"We'll take good care of him," Dr. Franklin said again, and this time the words seemed to settle into the room like a promise.

The Howard Johnson's sat just off the main road, its orange roof bright even under the gray drizzle. Inside, the air was warm and smelled faintly of coffee, fried clams, and the sweet vanilla of the ice cream freezer. A waitress in a crisp turquoise uniform led Bill and Jeanie to a booth near the window, the vinyl seats squeaking softly as they slid in.

Bill took off his hat and set it beside him. Jeanie folded her hands on the table, then unfolded them, then folded them again.

The waitress poured two coffees without asking. "Cream and sugar's right there, hon. I'll give you a minute."

When she walked away, the silence settled in — not awkward, just heavy, like a blanket they were both holding up with tired arms.

Jeanie stared out at the parking lot where the rain made tiny rings in the puddles. "I keep thinking," she said softly, "maybe we're overreacting. Maybe it's just… growing pains. Or nerves. Or something simple."

Bill nodded, though his jaw was tight. "Could be. Kids go through all kinds of things."

"Dr. Sherman said it might be nothing," Jeanie added quickly, as if stacking up reassurances might build a wall strong enough to hold back her fear. "And Jake's always been… dreamy. Off in his own world sometimes."

"Yeah," Bill said. "He's always been that way."

But they both knew this was different. They both knew it.

Jeanie wrapped her hands around the warm coffee cup. "I just keep hearing Clara's voice. 'My cousin had the same exact thing… turned out to be epilepsy.'" She swallowed. "I wish she'd never said that."

Bill reached across the table and covered her hand with his. "Let's not jump to that. Dr. Franklin said there are lots of explanations."

"I know," she whispered. "I know."

They sat quietly for a moment, listening to the soft clatter of dishes from the kitchen, the low hum of conversation from the other booths. The world around them felt strangely normal, as if nothing important were happening anywhere.

Jeanie forced a small smile. "I wonder how Emmett's doing."

That opened a gentler door between them.

Bill leaned back, letting out a breath that was almost a laugh. "Dad's probably entertaining him with those awful puns."

Jeanie's smile grew a little. "Or that trick where he pretends to pull a quarter out of your ear."

"He'll have Emmett convinced he's a magician by lunchtime."

"And your mother…" Jeanie shook her head fondly. "She'll have a whole tray of cupcakes cooling on the counter. You know how she gets when she has company."

"Especially grandkids," Bill said. "She'll let him lick the frosting bowl clean."

They both laughed — a soft, real laugh — and for a moment the weight lifted.

Then, just as quickly, it fell again.

The laughter faded, leaving behind a thin thread of guilt.

Jeanie looked down at her coffee. "How can we laugh when Jake's… when he's going through all this?"

Bill rubbed his forehead. "Because if we don't, we'll fall apart."

She nodded, eyes shining. "I just want him to be all right."

"I know," Bill said. "Me too."

The waitress returned with menus, but neither of them opened theirs.

"Take your time," she said kindly, sensing something she didn't need to understand.

When she walked away again, Jeanie reached for Bill's hand. "Do you think… do you think Dr. Franklin will come back and say it's nothing? That we worried ourselves sick for no reason?"

Bill squeezed her fingers. "I hope so. God, I hope so."

Outside, the drizzle thickened, streaking the window in long, wavering lines. Cars passed with their headlights on, their tires whispering over the wet pavement.

Inside the booth, Bill and Jeanie sat close, their shoulders touching, two parents holding each other up in the quiet space between fear and hope.

Bill ordered a club sandwich he barely touched. Jeanie picked at a grilled cheese until the bread went cold. The coffee sat between them, growing darker and more bitter as it cooled.

Finally Bill pushed his plate away. "Let's get some air."

Jeanie nodded, grateful for something to do besides sit and worry. They paid the check and stepped back out into the drizzle, which had softened to a mist so fine it felt like breath on the skin.

The University of Virginia campus lay just across the way — the Rotunda rising pale and domed against the gray sky, the Lawn stretching out in long, quiet symmetry. Students hurried past under umbrellas, their laughter and chatter drifting like a language from another world.

Bill and Jeanie walked slowly beneath the colonnades, their footsteps echoing on the wet brick. The white columns gleamed faintly in the damp light, and the air smelled of wet grass and old trees.

Jeanie slipped her arm through Bill's. "It's beautiful here."

"Always has been," he said. "Feels like a place where things turn out all right."

She leaned her head briefly against his shoulder. "Maybe Dr. Franklin will come back and say we worried ourselves sick over nothing."

Bill nodded. "Maybe he will."

They walked a little farther, past the student rooms with their wooden doors and brass numbers, past a professor in a tweed coat hurrying under an umbrella, past a group of students tossing a football despite the drizzle.

Bill stopped walking. He turned to her, brushing a damp strand of hair from her cheek. "We're doing the best we can. That's all anybody can do."

She nodded, but her eyes filled. "I just want him to be all right."

"I know," Bill said. "Me too."

They stood there for a moment under the colonnade, the mist drifting around them, the world moving on as if nothing were wrong.

Finally Bill said, "We should head back."

Jeanie took a breath, steadying herself. "Yes. It's time."

The Results

The neurology waiting room was quiet when Bill and Jeanie returned, the kind of quiet that made every sound — the turning of a magazine page, even a whisper — feel too loud.

They sat side by side in two stiff chairs upholstered in a pattern of green leaves. A clock on the wall ticked steadily, each second a small reminder of how slowly time could move when you needed it to hurry.

Jeanie clasped her hands in her lap. "Do you think he's scared?"

Bill shook his head gently. "He's braver than he knows."

A nurse passed by and offered them a polite smile — the kind that tried to reassure without promising anything. Jeanie watched her disappear around a corner.

Bill leaned forward, elbows on his knees. "Whatever the doctor says… we'll face it together."

Jeanie nodded, though her breath caught. "I know."

The clock ticked on.

Somewhere down the hall, behind closed doors, their son was undergoing the long, careful tests Dr. Franklin had described — tests meant to reveal what lay hidden beneath the surface, tests that would help the doctor understand the cause of Jake's episodes and headaches.

Tests that would lead, soon enough, to a truth no parent ever wants to hear.

Bill reached for Jeanie's hand. She took it, holding on tightly.

They waited.

The waiting room door opened with a soft click, and Dr. Franklin stepped inside. His expression was composed, but something in his eyes — a gravity deeper than before — made Jeanie's breath catch.

Bill and Jeanie both stood at once.

"Mr. and Mrs. Sonnett," he said quietly, "would you come with me, please?"

They followed him down the hall, their footsteps sounding too loud on the polished floor. The corridor seemed longer than it had that morning, the lights too bright, the air too still.

Inside his office, Dr. Franklin closed the door gently and gestured for them to sit. He remained standing for a moment, one hand resting on the back of his chair, as if choosing his words with great care.

Bill felt Jeanie's hand find his. He held it tightly.

Dr. Franklin sat down.

He folded his hands. Looked at them both.

And then he said it.

"The tests show that your son has a tumor in his brain."

The words hit like a blow — sharp, sudden, impossible. Jeanie inhaled sharply, a sound closer to a gasp than a breath. Bill felt the room tilt, as if the floor had dropped an inch beneath him.

Dr. Franklin continued, his voice steady but gentle. "The tests show a mass in the left temporal region. It's pressing on areas that control awareness and sensation. That explains the episodes you've been seeing… and the headaches."

Jeanie shook her head once, as if she hadn't heard correctly. "A… a tumor?"

"Yes," he said softly.

Bill swallowed hard. "Is it… is it cancer?"

"We don't know yet," Dr. Franklin said. "Some tumors in children are benign. Some are not. We won't know until it's removed and examined."

Removed.

The word landed with its own weight.

Jeanie's voice trembled. "Surgery?"

"Yes," he said. "He will need surgery. Soon."

Jeanie pressed a hand to her mouth. Tears spilled over her fingers.

Bill felt his heart hammering, a deep, painful thud in his chest. "What… what are the risks?"

Dr. Franklin didn't look away. "All brain surgery carries risks. Bleeding. Infection. Damage to surrounding tissue. But without surgery, the pressure will continue to increase. The episodes will worsen."

Jeanie whispered, "Oh God…"

Dr. Franklin leaned forward slightly, his voice low and steady. "I know this is overwhelming. I'm so sorry. But I want you to hear this clearly: many children come through this kind of surgery very well. We have an excellent neurosurgical team here. They've done this before."

Jeanie wiped her eyes with trembling fingers. "But he's just a little boy."

"I know," Dr. Franklin said. "And we're going to take the best possible care of him."

Bill stared at the floor for a long moment, trying to gather himself, trying to breathe. When he finally looked up, his voice was rough. "When… when do you want to do it?"

"As soon as possible," Dr. Franklin said. "I'd like to admit him today and schedule the operation for tomorrow morning."

Jeanie's breath broke. "Tomorrow?"

"Yes."

The clock on the wall ticked once. Twice. Three times.

Bill reached for Jeanie's hand again. She clung to him, her shoulders shaking.

Dr. Franklin waited, giving them space to absorb the blow.

When he finally spoke again, his voice was almost a whisper.

"I know this is not the news you hoped for. But you're not alone in this. We'll walk every step with you."

Jeanie stared at the doctor as if the world had tilted under her feet. Bill felt her hand trembling in his.

Dr. Franklin waited, giving them space to absorb the blow.

Bill swallowed hard, his voice rough. "Jeanie… do you agree we should go ahead? Have him admitted?"

Jeanie didn't trust her voice. She nodded — once, slowly — tears slipping down her cheeks.

Bill turned back to the doctor, steadying himself with a breath that felt too big for his chest. "All right," he said. "We'll… we'll talk to Jake."

Dr. Franklin nodded gently, rising from his chair. "Take whatever time you need. I'll have the nurse bring you to him when you're ready."

***

Saturday mornings at Ed and Oreen Sonnett's house had a rhythm all their own, and with Emmett staying for the weekend, the place felt livelier than usual.

The television — a sturdy black-and-white Zenith with rabbit-ear antennas wrapped in aluminum foil — glowed in the corner of the living room. On the screen, the familiar swirl of the *WTTG Channel 5* station ID faded into the bright, jangling theme of *Captain Kangaroo*. Emmett sat cross-legged on the braided rug, a bowl of cornflakes forgotten beside him, his eyes wide with delight.

Ed sat in his armchair, polishing his glasses with a handkerchief. "You know," he said, leaning toward Emmett, "I once met Captain Kangaroo."

Emmett turned, astonished. "You did not!"

"I surely did," Ed said, straight-faced. "He borrowed my scissors. Needed 'em to trim his bangs."

Oreen, passing through with a tray of freshly baked cupcakes, snorted. "Ed Sonnett, you never met that man in your life."

“Maybe not,” Ed admitted, “but I’d have lent him my scissors if he’d asked.”

Emmett giggled, then turned back to the TV as *Mighty Mouse* swooped across the screen on *WRC Channel 4*. The room filled with the bright, heroic fanfare.

Oreen set the cupcakes on the kitchen counter, the warm scent of vanilla drifting through the house. “Emmett, sweetheart, you want one of these after lunch?”

“Yes, ma’am!” he called, without looking away from the screen.

Ed winked at her. “He’s got his priorities straight.”

They had lunch early — grilled cheese sandwiches and tomato soup — and afterward Emmett returned to the living room for *Sky King* on *WMAL Channel 7*. Ed settled beside him, showing him how to make a coin “disappear” into thin air, then reappear behind his ear.

“Grandpa!” Emmett squealed. “How do you do that?”

“Trade secret,” Ed said, tapping the side of his nose.

The phone rang.

Oreen wiped her hands on her apron. “Ed, get that, would you?”

He rose, shuffled to the hallway, and lifted the receiver from its cradle.

“Sonnett residence… Well, hey there, son… Uh-huh… Uh-huh…”

His voice stayed steady, but his shoulders stiffened just slightly — a small, almost imperceptible tightening.

"Yes… yes, of course… We'll keep him as long as you need… All right… You tell Jeanie we're praying… Yes… All right, son. We love you too."

He hung up slowly.

When he stepped back into the living room, he put on a bright smile for Emmett. "Well now," he said, clapping his hands together, "good news! You get to stay the whole weekend with us."

"Really?" Emmett beamed. "All weekend?"

"All weekend," Ed said. "We'll have ourselves a grand time."

Emmett cheered and turned back to the TV, where *The Lone Ranger* was just beginning.

Ed caught Oreen's eye and gave a small nod toward the kitchen.

She followed him quietly.

In the kitchen, away from the sound of the television, Ed leaned against the counter, his face drawn.

"It's bad," he said softly. "Real bad."

Oreen pressed a hand to her chest. "Oh, Ed…"

"He didn't say much. But enough." He shook his head. "Our boy's hurting. Jeanie too."

Oreen's eyes filled. "And Jake?"

Ed swallowed. "They're admitting him today."

She closed her eyes, steadying herself. "Lord help them."

Ed reached for her hand. They stood there in the quiet kitchen, the smell of cupcakes still warm in the air, holding on to each other as the weight of the news settled over them.

The Earning

The noonday light slanted across the storefront windows on Main Street as Terry and Eddie stepped out of the barber shop and headed toward the clothing shop two doors down.

Eddie walked beside Terry in silence for half a block, his brow furrowed in that way Terry had come to recognize — the look of a boy thinking hard but unsure if he had the right to speak.

Finally Eddie cleared his throat. "Terry?"

"Yeah?"

Eddie kept his eyes on the sidewalk. "That house we went to. The Marigold place."

Terry nodded. "What about it?"

Eddie hesitated, then said, "You… you planning to go back?"

Terry slowed his pace a little. "I might. There's still a lot there to look through. Dr. Whitmore's got a list a mile long."

Eddie kicked at a loose bit of gravel. "It was… I dunno. Kinda spooky. But kinda… neat too."

Terry smiled. "That's about right."

Eddie risked a glance up at him. "If you go back… could I come? I mean, only if you want. I ain't trying to get in the way."

Terry stopped walking. "Eddie, you weren't in the way. You did fine."

"Terry," he said, "you don't have to do this."

Terry glanced over. "Do what?"

"Buy me stuff." Eddie kicked at a loose pebble on the sidewalk. "Clothes and all. I ain't… I ain't your responsibility."

Terry stopped walking. "Eddie, look at me."

Eddie hesitated, then lifted his eyes.

"You're staying with me for now," Terry said. "And you need clothes that fit. That's all this is."

"But it's your money," Eddie muttered. "Feels wrong."

Terry considered what Eddie had just said. "All right. Then let's make a deal."

Eddie blinked. "What kind of deal?"

"You want to earn your own way? Fine. You can. I've always got chores that need doing. Yard work. Splitting kindling. Helping me with carpentry projects. And that truck of mine—" he jerked a thumb toward the faded blue Ford parked at the curb— "she needs washing and waxing more than I care to admit."

Eddie's expression shifted — suspicion giving way to something like cautious hope. "You mean… I could earn money? For real?"

"For real," Terry said. "Fair pay for fair work."

Eddie looked down at his worn sneakers, then back up. "I can do that."

"I know you can."

They resumed walking, side by side this time.

When they reached the clothing store, Terry held the door open. "Come on. Let's get you fixed up."

Eddie stepped inside, still unsure, still shy — but no longer shrinking.

And for the first time in a long while, he felt the faint, unfamiliar warmth of someone believing he was worth the trouble.

They left the clothing store a few minutes later, Eddie carrying a small paper sack with his new things folded inside. The rain that had been threatening all morning had finally blown off, leaving the sidewalks damp and shining. Sunlight broke through the thinning clouds, warm and clean, and the air smelled of wet pavement and budding trees.

Terry glanced up at the sky, then over at Eddie.

"You ever been canoeing?"

Eddie blinked. "No, sir."

"Well," Terry said, a grin tugging at the corner of his mouth, "there's no time like the present."

He steered them toward the truck. Ten minutes later they were pulling up behind his father's house, where the old aluminum canoe rested upside down on sawhorses. Together they loaded it into the truck bed, along with two paddles and a pair of life jackets. Terry tied everything down with practiced knots, giving each rope a firm tug before climbing back into the cab.

They drove only a short distance — to the quiet end of Luray Avenue, where a narrow bridge crossed a calm stretch of the Shenandoah. Terry parked beneath the shade of a sycamore, and the two of them carried the canoe down to the water's edge.

The river was peaceful, the surface smooth except for the slow, steady drift of the current. Sunlight glimmered on the ripples like scattered coins.

Terry steadied the canoe while Eddie climbed into the bow, then pushed off and settled himself in the stern.

"Ever heard of a J-stroke?" Terry asked.

Eddie shook his head.

Terry dipped his paddle into the water, demonstrating the long pull and the subtle outward flick that kept the canoe straight. "Like that. Smooth and easy."

They pushed out into the center of the river. Neither of them spoke. The only sounds were the soft dip of the paddles, the hush of water sliding past the hull, and a distant woodpecker tapping somewhere along the bank.

Eddie sat very still in the bow, his shoulders relaxed, his eyes wide and drinking in everything — the bright water, the green banks, the quiet that felt like a blanket around them. Terry watched him for a moment, then looked back to the river, letting the silence do its work.

For the first time since he'd met the boy, Terry saw Eddie at rest — not braced, not wary, not waiting for the next blow to fall. Just… present.

That night, after Eddie had gone to bed and the house had settled into its familiar creaks and sighs, Terry lay awake longer than usual. The day had been full — heavier than he'd expected — and his mind kept circling back to the boy asleep in the next room, to the clothes folded neatly on the chair, to the quiet hope he'd seen flicker in Eddie's eyes.

When he finally drifted off, the dream came quickly.

It was a dream that would stay in his memory for a long time.

He and Eddie were in a small wooden boat on the Shenandoah River, the water smooth as glass beneath them. Mist curled along the surface, soft and silver, and the current carried them forward without effort. Eddie sat in the bow, quiet and watchful, his hands resting on the gunwales.

Terry dipped a paddle into the water, guiding them gently downstream.

Then he saw her.

A woman standing on the riverbank, half-veiled by the morning mist. She didn't wave, didn't call out — she simply lifted her hand in a quiet beckoning, as if she'd been waiting for him.

Terry felt no fear, only a strange, calm certainty. He paddled toward her.

When the boat touched the shore, the woman stepped lightly into it, her dress brushing the water's edge without getting wet. She sat opposite him, her face serene, her eyes steady and knowing.

"My name is Alethea," she said.

Her voice was soft, but it carried over the river like a bell.

Terry opened his mouth to speak, but the dream shifted — the mist thickened, the river brightened, and the woman's face seemed to glow with a quiet, sorrowful light.

Then he awoke.

The room was dark, the house still. But the dream clung to him — clear, whole, and unsettling in its certainty.

"Alethea."

He whispered the name into the quiet, as if testing its weight.

And he felt that the dream meant something. That it wasn't finished with him yet.

The Vigil

After Jake's surgery, a nurse led Bill and Jeanie down a narrow hallway that smelled faintly of antiseptic and warm linen. The lights were low. The sound of their footsteps echoed loudly.

"Just in here," she whispered, as if sound itself might disturb him.

Bill and Jeanie stepped into the small recovery room.

Jake lay on the narrow bed, his head wrapped in thick white bandages, an IV taped to his arm. His skin looked pale against the sheets, almost translucent. A slow, steady beep from the monitor marked his heartbeat, each sound a tiny reassurance.

Jeanie pressed a hand to her mouth.

Bill felt something inside him twist.

Jake's eyelids fluttered, then opened just a sliver. His gaze drifted unfocused across the room before settling — slowly, heavily — on his parents.

"Mom?" His voice was thin, raspy. Barely audible.

Jeanie moved to his side at once. "I'm right here, sweetheart."

Jake blinked, trying to understand where he was. "It… hurts."

"I know," she whispered, brushing his hand with her fingertips. "The doctor said that's normal."

Bill stood on the other side of the bed, one hand gripping the metal rail. "You did real good, son. Real good."

Jake's eyes drifted closed again, exhaustion pulling him under.

A soft knock sounded at the door.

Dr. Franklin stepped in, his expression gentle but composed. "He's doing well," he said quietly. "The surgery went as expected. We were able to remove the mass completely."

Jeanie let out a breath she didn't realize she'd been holding. Bill closed his eyes for a moment, steadying himself.

Dr. Franklin continued, "He'll be very tired for the next day or so. Some confusion is normal. Headaches too. We'll keep a close watch on him."

"Is he… out of danger?" Bill asked, his voice low.

"For now, yes," the doctor said. "The next twenty-four hours are important. We'll monitor for swelling, infection, any changes in his responses. But so far, everything looks promising."

Jeanie nodded, tears slipping silently down her cheeks.

Dr. Franklin rested a hand briefly on the bed rail. "You can stay with him a little longer, but visiting hours end soon. He needs rest."

When the doctor left, the room felt smaller, quieter — just the three of them and the soft hum of machines.

Jake stirred again, whispering something they couldn't quite catch. Jeanie leaned close, gently touching his cheek with trembling fingers.

Bill watched them, his heart full and aching.

After a long while, Jeanie said softly, "Bill… you should go home tonight. Get some rest."

Bill shook his head. "I'm not leaving you here alone."

"I'll be all right," she said. "I want to stay. I need to stay."

He hesitated, torn between exhaustion and the instinct to protect them both.

Jeanie touched his arm. "And Bill… on Monday, you should go in to work."

He blinked. "Jeanie, I'm not thinking about work right now."

"I know," she said. "But you need something steady. Something normal. And maybe you'll sell a car. Might give you a little lift."

Bill let out a breath, half a sigh, half a laugh. "A lift," he repeated. "Feels like I could use one."

"You will," she said. "And it'll help you keep your feet under you. We both need that."

Bill looked at her for a long moment — at her tired eyes, her quiet resolve, the way she was holding herself together for all three of them.

"All right," he said finally. "I'll go."

She nodded, relieved.

He withdrew a few bills from his wallet and pressed them into her hand. "For a taxi to a motel. Don't walk. Not tonight."

She closed her fingers around the money. "I won't."

Bill looked at Jake one last time — the bandages, the stillness, the small rise and fall of his chest — then leaned down and kissed Jeanie's forehead.

"I'll call when I get home," he said softly.

She squeezed his hand. "Drive safe."

Bill walked down the hallway, the hush of the hospital settling around him like a weight. At the elevator he paused, rubbing a hand over his face. He could still see Jake's pale skin, the bandages, the slow rise and fall of his chest. He could still see Jeanie sitting beside him, steady in a way he wasn't sure he could match.

The memory of their first child flickered through him — that tiny life they hadn't been able to save. The ache of it rose up sharp and familiar, and this time he didn't push the thought away. *If there is a God…* He swallowed hard. *If there is a God, please keep my boy safe. Please bring him back to us. Don't let us lose another.*

He stood there a moment, eyes closed, tears forming, letting the silent prayer settle in his chest. They had done everything they could — found the best doctor, asked every question, signed every form. The rest was beyond him. Whether anyone was listening or not, he had to trust. He had to.

As he stepped into the elevator, Bill straightened his shoulders. There were things he *could* do: get home safely, call Jeanie, show up on Monday like she asked. Keep moving. Keep steady. And there were things he couldn't — the healing happening inside their boy's head, the long hours ahead, the uncertainty. The fear.

He exhaled slowly, letting the doors close in front of him.

For tonight, trust — in God, in the doctors, in something beyond his reach — would have to be enough.

A Small Turning

Terry pulled into the lot just as the late-day sun was catching the chrome on the new models lined up in front of the showroom. Eddie sat beside him, taking everything in with that alert, hungry look he had — the kind of look that said he was memorizing the world as fast as it came at him.

They walked toward the showroom, Eddie trailing a step behind, eyes wide at the polished cars under the bright lights.

Eddie had never seen so many brand-new cars up close, not all at once, not gleaming like this. The chrome, the paint, the spotless windows — it was like stepping into another world.

He leaned in close to Terry and whispered, almost afraid someone might overhear, "You really gonna buy one of these?"

Terry glanced down at him. "Thinking about it."

Bill spotted them through the window in his office and came out with a wave. "Well, look who's here," he said, grinning. "Terry, good to see you. And who's this young man?"

"This is my buddy Eddie," Terry said, giving the boy a gentle nudge forward. "Thought I'd bring him along."

Bill shook Eddie's hand. "Glad to meet you."

Eddie nodded, shy but steady. "Nice to meet you, sir."

Terry cleared his throat. "I've been thinking about what you said the other day. About a trade-in."

Bill's eyebrows lifted. "Oh yeah?"

"Yeah. Figured it wouldn't hurt to take a look."

Bill clapped his hands together. "Well, let's get your truck around back. The boys'll give it a once-over, see what we can offer you."

Terry handed over the keys. "She runs great. I've kept up with everything myself. Just needs a paint job."

"I know you take care of your things," Bill said. "That helps the value."

They walked toward the showroom, Eddie trailing a step behind, eyes wide at the polished cars under the bright lights.

"I don't know if I want another truck," Terry said. "Been thinking maybe it's time for a car. Something a little more… presentable."

Bill chuckled. "Presentable, huh?"

Terry shrugged, a little sheepish. "If I want to take a lady friend out, a car makes a better impression than a pickup."

Bill nodded. "You're not wrong."

Inside, the smell of new upholstery and floor wax filled the air. Bill leaned against a desk and looked over at Eddie.

"How old are you, son?"

"Sixteen," Eddie said.

"That's perfect," Bill said. "You ever think about Scouts? I help lead a troop — we do a lot of camping and canoeing."

Eddie's eyes flickered with interest. "I never been in Scouts."

"Well, we've got a campout next weekend. There's a chance I might not make it — my boy just had surgery, and he'll probably be coming home around then — but Joe Driggs will be there. Good man. And Terry, you're welcome to come along too."

Terry looked up sharply. "How is your son?"

Bill's expression softened. "Jake's doing all right. Tired. Sore. But the doctor says the surgery went as expected. We'll know more in a few days."

"I'm glad to hear it," Terry said quietly.

Bill nodded once, grateful.

Just then one of the mechanics poked his head in. "We'll have numbers for you in a bit, Bill."

"Thanks, Charlie."

Bill turned back to Terry. "Now, if you're thinking car… I've got something you ought to see."

He led them to a gleaming, new 1961 Chevrolet Bel Air, two-tone blue and white, the chrome trim catching the light like jewelry.

Terry let out a low whistle. "Now that's sharp."

"Drives like a dream," Bill said. "And if you wanted, you could drive it off the lot today."

Terry walked around it slowly, hand trailing along the fender. "I definitely want it," he said. "But I need to check with my bank first."

"No problem, my friend."

Eddie stood beside him, still staring at the car. "It's real nice," he murmured.

Terry smiled. "Yeah, it is."

Bill clapped Eddie on the shoulder. "And you think about that campout. We'd be glad to have you."

Eddie nodded, a spark of something hopeful in his eyes. "I'd like to go."

"Good," Bill said. "We'll make it happen."

The three of them stood there a moment — Terry with a new car in his sights, Eddie with a new world opening up, and Bill carrying the weight of his son's recovery but still offering what he could.

A small, ordinary moment. But one that nudged all their lives a little further forward.

PART III

THE TRUTH EMERGES

When Good News Comes Calling

Terry had just come in from the garage, hands still smelling faintly of oil and cold metal, when the phone rang. He wiped his palms on a rag and picked up the receiver.

"Hello?"

"Terry, it's Whitmore."

The professor's voice always carried a kind of clipped excitement, as though he lived in a world where discoveries were waiting just behind the next sentence. Today, though, there was something extra in it — a brightness, a suppressed triumph.

"I've got news," Whitmore said.

Terry straightened. "About the book?"

"Yes. I've sent it on to a colleague in Charlottesville. A government cryptologist. Brilliant fellow. Works quietly, keeps to himself. The university uses him from time to time when something… unusual comes across our desks."

Terry felt a small, sharp thrill. "And he's willing to look at it?"

"Oh, more than willing. He's agreed to take a crack at it."

Whitmore paused, clearly pleased with himself. "Get it? Crack the code?"

Terry closed his eyes. "Lord, Professor."

Whitmore chuckled. "All right, all right. Bad joke. But he's already begun. Says it may take a few days, but he's confident there's a pattern in the cipher. Looks like a simple substitution code."

Terry felt his pulse quicken. "So we'll know soon."

"Yes. And when we do, I want you to be the first to hear it. You and the boy. I'll be back in touch very soon."

Terry swallowed. "Eddie'll be glad to know. He's been thinking about it a lot."

"As he should," Whitmore said. "It's a remarkable piece of history you two stumbled into."

They spoke a few minutes more — practical things, timelines, the professor's assurance that the university would cover the cryptologist's fee — and then Terry hung up.

He stood there a moment, the quiet of the house settling around him. Outside, the late afternoon sun slanted across the yard, catching the dust motes in the air. Somewhere down the street a dog barked. Ordinary sounds. Ordinary day.

But something had shifted.

He felt it — the way you feel a storm coming long before the clouds gather.

He grabbed his jacket and headed for the truck. Eddie would want to hear this. And there was something good about telling the boy in person, seeing his face light up, watching that spark of hope catch fire again.

As he backed out of the driveway, Terry realized he was smiling.

The truth — whatever it was — was finally on its way.

Terry found Eddie exactly where he said he would be—at the Talleys' place, helping Mr. Talley stack firewood.

The boy's face lit up when Terry told him about Whitmore's call — not wildly, just that quiet spark he got when hope surprised him. They talked about it on the drive home, Eddie asking careful questions, Terry answering what he could. By the time they pulled into the driveway, the sun was gone and the house felt settled again, the excitement tucked away but still warm between them.

That evening, when Terry reached for the phone to call Joe Driggs, Eddie was already at the kitchen table with a Field & Stream, pretending not to listen.

Joe answered on the second ring. "Driggs here."

"Joe, it's Terry. About the campout this weekend. Eddie and I want to join, if that's okay — what do we need to bring?"

"Of course it's okay. Bill Sonnett told me you would probably be in touch," Joe said. "And as far as what you need to bring, the troop supplies the big stuff. Tents, cots, food. We've got all that covered."

"What about the boys?" Terry asked.

"Sleeping bags, canteen, flashlights, a jacket, and five dollars each. That's it. We meet at Chimney Field Saturday morning and carpool from there."

Terry nodded, though Joe couldn't see it. He repeated, "Sleeping bags, canteen, flashlights, a jacket, and five dollars," and added, "I can haul gear in the back of my pickup if you need it—that is if I haven't traded it in on a new car I've been eyeing."

Joe chuckled. "It's about time you traded in that old pickup."

Terry grinned. "Well, that's still up in the air."

"Either way," Joe said, "we'll make it work. And tell Eddie we're glad to have him. Good group of boys this year."

Eddie pretended not to be listening, but the magazine slipped a little in his hands.

After they hung up, Terry turned to him. "You hear all that?"

Eddie nodded. "I think so—at least, what you said. Sleeping bag, flashlight, jacket, and five dollars."

He grinned.

"I got a jacket," he said. "And I can get the five dollars. I'll mow Mrs. Talley's yard again."

"You don't have to do that," Terry said gently. "I've got you covered."

Eddie shook his head. "I want to pay my own way."

Terry didn't argue. He just nodded, respecting the boy's pride.

"We'll find you a good flashlight," Terry said. "Doesn't have to be fancy."

Terry leaned back in his chair. "You excited?"

Eddie shrugged, but his voice betrayed him. "Yeah. I am."

"Good," Terry said. "It'll be a good weekend. I'm sure Joe runs a tight ship. And the boys are decent."

Eddie looked down at the magazine again, but this time he wasn't pretending. He was imagining it — the tents, the fire, the woods, the chance to be just another kid for a while.

Terry watched him, feeling something warm settle in his chest. The boy had been through so much, carried so much. A simple campout shouldn't feel like a second chance at life — but for Eddie, it did.

"Saturday morning," Terry said. "Chimney Field. We'll be there."

Eddie nodded, and for the first time in a long while, he looked like he believed it.

Life was already slipping into a rhythm — school for Eddie, work for Terry — but the promise of the cryptologist's findings and the upcoming campout hovered in the background as coming changes.

The Gift of Seeing

By Wednesday Jake had improved so much that he was allowed to go home from the hospital. The bandage around his head made him look smaller somehow, and another wrapped his left hand where the IV had been.

Terry heard the good news and phoned Bill.

"I bet you're glad to have Jake back at home," Terry said.

Bill let out a breath that sounded like it had been waiting all week to escape. "Absolutely. I'll be honest, Terry — I didn't realize how tense I've been until we finally got him home."

There was a pause, the kind that comes when a man is trying not to let his voice break.

"You want me to stop by tomorrow?" Terry asked. "Bring anything?"

"No, no," Bill said quickly. "We've got food stacked to the ceiling. But… if you'd like to come by, let's make it Friday after work. I think Jake would like that. He's been asking about you."

Terry smiled. "I'll be there."

By Friday Jake was feeling noticeably better, though still pale and moving carefully. The big easy chair in the living room — the one usually reserved for his father — had been stuffed with pillows and now marked the full extent of his mobility. On the table beside him sat a glass of water with a bending straw, the kind you didn't have to lift your head to use.

He was actually able to enjoy breakfast.

After he had eaten, his mother said, "Jake, honey. I want to introduce you to Mrs. Jackson. She'll be staying with you today while I'm out."

The woman beside his mother was Black, maybe in her late forties, dressed in the plain white of a home-care aide. She gave Jake a small, professional nod. When she stepped forward, he noticed the watch on her wrist turned inward for easy checking — just like Dr. Sherman.

Mrs. Jackson checked Jake's temperature and took his pulse. She asked if he'd like her to bring him one of his books.

"Just my drawing pad and pencils," he said.

She brought them to him, and before long she made note of how fast he was working — quick, sure strokes, his face intent despite the fatigue.

Later in the afternoon he asked for his watercolor set. Mrs. Jackson hesitated, but seeing how alert and steady he was, she handed it over. He worked quietly, absorbed, until nearly time for his family to come home.

Then, worn out, he fell asleep in the chair.

When Jeanie, Bill, and Emmett came through the door, Mrs. Jackson put a finger to her lips and motioned them over. Jake's drawing pad had slipped from his lap and lay face-up on the floor.

All three of them stopped cold.

It was a watercolor painting of the Shenandoah Valley — not only expertly drawn, but bright and luminous, as if the late afternoon sun were caught inside the page. The church spires and the courthouse roofline rose above the trees. The Blue Ridge Mountains stood in the distance. The highway curved toward the bridge, and the Shenandoah

River ran beneath it in soft, glowing washes of color. And on the river, in shadow but unmistakable, was a man in a boat.

It was beautiful. It was, simply, a masterpiece.

Jeanie and Bill thanked Mrs. Jackson and quietly walked her to the door.

That evening Terry and Eddie dropped by to check on Jake. He brightened when he saw them.

Terry stepped forward, his face softening when he got a good look at Jake propped in the chair.

"I'm real glad to see you feeling better," he said. "You've been through a rough ordeal, kid. A real one."

Jake shrugged a little, embarrassed but pleased.

Terry continued, "By the way — I showed that copy you made for me to a history professor from the university. Really smart guy. And you know what he said? He was amazed. Absolutely amazed."

Jake blinked, surprised.

"They're gonna use your copy for their research," Terry said, grinning. "Said it was the best rendering he'd ever seen."

"Really?" Jake whispered. "I just… I wanted to make it good for you, Terry. I'm glad they liked it."

Eddie squinted at the bandage wrapped around Jake's head. "You look like one of those fortune-telling guys," he said. "You know — the ones with the turbans."

Jake smiled — afraid to laugh because it still hurt — and whispered, "I see in your future, the stars are in your favor."

Everyone burst out laughing. Everyone except Jake, who winced but kept smiling.

"Sounds like you're feeling pretty good, son," Jeanie said.

Bill, Jeanie, Emmett, Terry, and Eddie all sat down, and Bill carefully passed around Jake's new painting. They were amazed at the detail and the perspective. The more they looked, the more things they saw.

Bill said, "This one's sure to win the contest."

Emmett leaned in. "Well, I'll be a monkey's uncle," he said. "I think that guy in the canoe looks exactly like Mr. Miller."

Terry took the pad, studying the tiny figure for a long moment.

"Well I'll be an uncle's monkey," he said. "That's me all right. Flat-top haircut and all. Fantastic job, Jake."

Jake stirred a little at the sound of their voices. His eyes opened halfway, heavy with sleep, but he managed a faint smile. He didn't say anything — just closed his eyes again and let out a slow breath.

Terry, still holding the drawing pad, was reminded of his dream.

"Jake," he said softly, "why did you put me in your picture?"

But Jake was already asleep again, his breathing slow and even.

He knew he was going to be better really soon.

The Campout

Saturday morning broke clear and cool, the kind of early-spring day that promised warmth by noon but still held a bite in the air. Terry pulled into Chimney Field a few minutes before eight, his pickup rattling slightly as he eased into the gravel lot. Eddie sat beside him, clutching his rolled sleeping bag like it might try to run off if he loosened his grip.

A handful of boys were already there, tossing a baseball back and forth while their parents chatted near the cars. Joe Driggs stood by the troop trailer, clipboard in hand, calling out names as each boy arrived.

"There's Joe," Terry said. "Let's check in."

Eddie nodded, swallowing hard. He wasn't scared — not exactly — but he was alert in that way he always was around new groups, as if waiting to see which way the wind would blow.

Joe spotted them and waved. "Morning, Terry. Morning, Eddie."

"Morning, sir," Eddie said.

Joe checked his list. "You're all set. Sleeping bag, jacket, flashlight?"

"Yes, sir."

"Good. We'll load your things in the trailer. You can ride with me and Terry."

Eddie's shoulders eased a little.

Tommy Smith arrived a few minutes later, big for his age, loud, full of swagger. He hopped out of his father's station wagon holding a flashlight with a red lens and a canvas strap. He swung it around like a prize.

"Look at this, fellas," Tommy said. "Army-issue. My uncle gave it to me. You can't buy these in stores."

A couple boys crowded around, admiring it. Eddie hung back, but Tommy noticed him anyway.

"You ever seen one like this?" Tommy asked, holding it out.

Eddie nodded. "It's real nice."

Tommy grinned, pleased. "Bet you wish you had one."

Eddie shrugged. "Maybe someday."

Tommy laughed and tucked it into his belt like a sidearm.

By nine o'clock, the cars were loaded and the boys piled in. Eddie rode in the back seat of Joe's station wagon, between two younger Scouts who were arguing about who could paddle a canoe faster. Terry sat up front with Joe, window cracked, the cool air rushing in.

The drive to the campground took nearly an hour, winding through the foothills, past farms and budding orchards. Eddie stared out the window, watching the landscape roll by — the pale green of new leaves, the shimmer of the river glimpsed through the trees, the way the mountains rose and fell like ocean waves.

When they arrived, the boys spilled out of the cars, stretching their legs and shouting to one another. The campsite sat in a clearing near the water, ringed by tall pines that whispered in the breeze.

Joe clapped his hands. "All right, listen up! Tents first, then we'll get the fire going. Let's move."

The boys paired off, hauling canvas tents and metal poles from the trailer. Eddie worked with a quiet, serious boy named Mark, and the two of them managed to get their tent up without much trouble. Terry watched from a distance, pleased to see Eddie fitting in.

By noon, the camp was set. The boys ate sandwiches and apples, then headed down to the riverbank for canoeing. Eddie hesitated at first, but when Terry nudged him, he stepped into the canoe with Mark and another boy. They pushed off, paddles dipping into the water with soft, rhythmic splashes.

Eddie's face changed out there — loosened, brightened. He laughed once, a short, surprised sound, as if he hadn't expected it.

Later, around the fire, the boys roasted hot dogs and marshmallows and told stories. Tommy bragged about his uncle's time in the Army. Mark talked about catching a catfish "this big." Eddie listened, smiling, letting out a laugh or a nod, his only words a shy 'right' or 'wow' now and again.

For the first time in a long while, he looked like a boy among boys.

As the fire burned low and the stars came out, Terry leaned back on his elbows, watching Eddie across the circle. The boy was sitting with Mark and two others, passing around a bag of marshmallows, his face lit by the flickering glow.

Terry felt something settle in him — a quiet hope, a sense that maybe, just maybe, Eddie was finding his place.

He didn't know yet that the next morning would test the boy in ways neither of them could imagine.

But for now, the night was peaceful, the fire warm, and the river whispering softly in the dark.

The Accusation

The sun was barely up when the first shouts broke across the campground.

Terry had just poured himself a cup of coffee from the percolator when he heard Tommy Smith yelling near the tents. A few boys came running, half-dressed, hair sticking up, the kind of early-morning confusion that comes from sleeping outdoors.

Terry set down his cup and walked toward the noise. Joe Driggs was already there, calm but alert, clipboard tucked under his arm.

Tommy stood in front of his tent, face red, fists clenched. "Somebody stole my flashlight!" he shouted. "It was right here in my tent last night!"

A few boys murmured, glancing at one another.

Joe held up a hand. "All right, let's slow down. When did you last see it?"

"Before bed," Tommy said. "I put it right by my sleeping bag. And now it's gone."

One of the younger boys piped up, "Maybe you misplaced it."

Tommy rounded on him. "I didn't misplace it! Somebody took it."

His eyes swept the group, searching for a target. They landed on Eddie.

"You," Tommy said, pointing. "You were looking at it yesterday. You said you wished you had one like it."

Eddie froze. "I didn't take anything."

Tommy stepped closer. "You snuck into my tent. I know you did."

"I didn't," Eddie said, voice small but steady.

A few boys whispered. Terry caught fragments — "You know what he did before…" and "He's been in trouble…"

Joe's expression tightened. "Tommy, that's enough. We don't accuse people without proof."

Tommy crossed his arms. "Well, he's the only one who wanted it."

Eddie's face went pale. He looked at Terry, not pleading, just… lost.

Joe stepped forward. "Eddie, come with me a minute."

Terry followed them behind the mess tent, out of earshot of the others. Eddie stood stiffly, hands at his sides.

Joe spoke gently. "Son, Tommy says you took his flashlight. I need to ask you straight — did you?"

"No, sir," Eddie whispered. "I didn't touch it."

Terry could see the fear in the boy's eyes — not fear of punishment, but fear of being believed.

Joe nodded slowly. "All right. Then we're going to clear this up. I want you to dump out your duffel bag so we can show everyone you don't have it."

Eddie hesitated. Not because he was guilty — Terry could see that — but because the humiliation of being asked to prove his innocence cut deep.

Still, he knelt and unzipped the bag.

He turned it over.

Clothes spilled out. A rolled-up jacket. A paperback book. A pair of socks. A small tin of matches.

And then—

A flashlight. Tommy's flashlight. It hit the ground with a dull thud.

Eddie stared at it as if it were a snake. His mouth opened, but no sound came out.

Joe's face went still.

Terry felt something inside him drop — not doubt, but dread. He was certain Eddie hadn't taken it. He knew it as surely as he knew his own name. But the evidence lay there on the ground, cold and undeniable.

Behind them, a few boys had drifted closer, whispering.

"I knew it…"

"He stole it…"

"Just like before…"

Eddie's shoulders curled inward. He looked smaller than he had in months.

Joe cleared his throat. "All right," he said quietly. "Let's give this a minute. Eddie, go sit by the fire. Terry, stay with him. I'll talk to Tommy."

Eddie nodded, numb, and walked away.

Terry followed, his heart heavy. He sat beside the boy on a fallen log. Eddie stared at the dirt, hands clenched in his lap.

“I didn’t take it,” he whispered. “I swear.”

“I know,” Terry said. And he meant it.

But the morning had already turned. The easy warmth of the campout was gone, replaced by a tension that hung in the air like a storm waiting to break.

The boys went through the motions of breakfast, but the easy chatter of the night before was gone. Eddie sat apart from the others, knees drawn up, staring at the ashes of the fire as if trying to disappear into them.

Terry stayed close, not hovering, just present. Joe Driggs moved quietly through the camp, talking to boys one by one, gathering what scraps of information he could. But nothing changed the fact that Tommy’s flashlight had been found in Eddie’s duffel.

By midmorning, the tension had become a living thing.

At one point Terry noticed Mark, Eddie’s tent mate, walking toward the tree line beyond the tents with Tommy. Mark looked uneasy, glancing back toward camp as if he wished he were anywhere else. Tommy walked beside him with that same swagger he’d had all morning, the kind that came from knowing the crowd was on his side.

Terry nudged Joe. “Something’s going on over there.”

Joe followed his gaze. “I’ll check it out.”

He moved quietly toward the trees, boots soft on the pine needles.

Behind the trees, Mark’s voice trembled, but he pushed the words out anyway.

“Tommy, I can’t keep quiet. I saw what you did.”

Tommy stiffened. "What are you talking about?"

"I was awake last night," Mark said, voice shaking but determined. "Eddie was asleep. I heard something outside the tent and thought it was a raccoon. But it was you. I saw your shadow first, then you unzipped the flap real slow."

Tommy's jaw tightened.

"You crawled in," Mark continued, "and you had your flashlight in your hand. I saw the strap. You knelt by Eddie's bag and put it inside. Then you left and walked off like nothing happened."

Tommy grabbed Mark's arm and twisted it up behind his back. Mark gasped.

"Shut up," Tommy hissed. "That kid needs to be thrown out. Everybody knows what he is. And you're not telling anybody anything. You hear me?"

Mark winced. "You're hurting me…"

"Good. Maybe that'll help you remember to keep your mouth shut."

A branch snapped.

Both boys froze.

Joe Driggs stepped into the clearing, arms folded, expression carved from stone.

"Okay, boys," he said. "I heard it all."

Tommy's hand dropped instantly. Mark stumbled away, rubbing his arm.

Joe didn't raise his voice. He didn't need to. "Tommy, you're coming with me. Mark, you too."

Tommy's bravado drained out of him like water from a cracked bucket. He followed Joe back toward camp, shoulders hunched, steps dragging.

When they reached the fire circle, Eddie looked up — wary, braced for more humiliation.

Joe stopped in front of him. "Eddie," he said, "we owe you an apology. Tommy has something to say."

Tommy swallowed. His voice was barely audible. "I… I put the flashlight in your bag. I'm sorry."

A few boys gasped. Others stared at the ground, ashamed of the bad things they had been saying about Eddie.

Eddie blinked, stunned. "Why?"

Tommy shrugged helplessly. "I don't know. I just… I didn't want you here."

The silence that followed was long and heavy.

Then Eddie did something no one expected.

He stood up.

He looked Tommy in the eye — not angry, not triumphant, just steady.

"People can change," Eddie said quietly. "Maybe you can too."

Tommy's face crumpled. He nodded once, then turned away, shoulders shaking.

Joe put a hand on Eddie's shoulder. "You handled that like a man," he said softly.

And for the first time all weekend, the boys looked at Eddie not with suspicion, but with something closer to respect.

Terry watched him, feeling a swell of pride so deep it surprised him.

The truth had emerged — painfully, slowly, but unmistakably.

And Eddie, for the first time in his life, had stood in the light of it without flinching.

Magic

Monday, Terry took the morning off and after Eddie left for school he drove to the high school, the sun just clearing the ridge behind the football field. The halls were mostly quiet except for an occasional student dashing late to class. He signed in at the office and waited outside Principal Robert Wood's door, hands in his pockets, feeling the weight of what he was about to take on.

Mr. Wood waved him in. He was a tall man with a thinning hairline and the tired, watchful eyes of someone who had seen more than his share of boys like Eddie.

"You want to talk about Edward, I presume," Wood said, motioning to a chair.

Terry sat. "Yes, I do. Thank you for taking the time to see me."

Wood pulled a thin folder from a stack. "Edward's not a bad kid," he began, "but he's drifting. Chronic absences. Missing assignments. Keeps to himself. Doesn't cause trouble unless someone corners him, but he doesn't walk away either."

Terry nodded. "Eddie (that's what we call him) is a loner."

"Very much so," Wood said. "Bright enough, but closed off. Hard to reach."

"At least he's not in with the wrong crowd," Terry said. "He's not running wild."

"No," Wood agreed. "But he's not headed anywhere either."

Terry leaned forward. "I'm going to stay on top of this. Make sure he gets to school every day. Homework done. No trouble. I've already seen improvement."

Wood studied him for a long moment, weighing the sincerity. "If you're willing to put in the time, I'll do everything I can on my end."

Terry stood, shook his hand and thanked him, and started toward the door. Then he paused.

"One more thing," he said. "Eddie's… guarded. Closed up tight. Is there anything you'd suggest to help him open up? Feel safe enough to talk?"

Wood leaned back, thinking. "A dog," he said finally. "Some kids won't talk to people, but they'll talk to a dog. And a dog doesn't judge. I've seen a pet dog bring a child out of their shell."

Terry nodded slowly. "All right. I'll see what I can do."

Eddie came home that afternoon to find Terry already there, sitting at the kitchen table with a cup of coffee.

"Put your bookbag down," Terry said. "Grab a quick snack. We're going somewhere."

Eddie blinked. "Where?"

"You'll see."

They drove across town, past the river and the feed store, until Terry turned into the humane shelter. Eddie's eyes widened, and for the first time in days, he acted like a kid who was excited about Christmas.

Inside, the dogs barked and whined and scrambled at the cages. Eddie moved from kennel to kennel, kneeling, talking softly, studying each dog like he was trying to understand them.

Then he saw the beagle puppy — long ears, worried eyes, tail thumping like a drum.

"This one," Eddie whispered. "This is him."

Terry smiled. "All right then. What's his name?"

Eddie thought for a moment. "Since he looks like the Peanuts dog in the funny papers, I'll call him Snoopy."

Back home, Eddie was all motion — feeding Snoopy, walking him, showing him every corner of the yard. Terry helped him build a doghouse, though Eddie kept glancing toward the house like he already knew he wouldn't want Snoopy sleeping outside.

That night, when it was time to put the dog out, Eddie hesitated. "He'll be scared," he said. "He should stay with me."

Terry didn't argue. "All right. Your room, then."

Snoopy followed Eddie upstairs like he'd been doing it his whole life.

The next morning, Eddie's shout shook the house.

Terry hurried upstairs. Snoopy had found one of Eddie's sneakers and chewed it to pieces — strings, rubber, everything. Eddie, startled and angry, lashed out and struck the dog. Snoopy yelped and cowered in the corner, trembling and whimpering.

The sound hung in the air.

Eddie froze. His face changed — anger collapsing into horror, then something deeper. Recognition. He recognized that posture. He'd been in that posture.

And in that instant, he saw himself from the outside.

Not as a kid defending himself. Not as someone trying to be tough. But as a boy who had just made a smaller, weaker creature afraid of him.

A flash of his father — the stance, the anger, the sudden strike — hit him like a cold wind.

"I'm not going to be like him," Eddie whispered to himself. "I'm not."

He knelt, hands shaking, and gathered the trembling puppy into his arms. Snoopy pressed his face into Eddie's chest, trusting him instantly, and that trust broke something open.

"I'm sorry," Eddie whispered. "I'm sorry, boy."

Terry stood in the doorway, saying nothing. Eddie needed to come to this on his own.

Later, Eddie came downstairs with the puppy tucked under his arm.

"Terry?" he said quietly.

"Yeah?"

"The dog's name isn't Snoopy anymore."

Terry waited.

"His name is Magic."

Terry nodded. "That's a good name."

Eddie looked down at the puppy, who licked his chin. "Yeah," he said. "It is."

As time went on, Magic settled into the house as if he'd been waiting for it his whole short life. Within a week he knew the sound of Eddie's footsteps on the stairs, the scrape of Terry's boots on the porch, the rattle of kibble in the tin by the back door. He followed Eddie everywhere — room to room, yard to yard — a small, warm shadow with a tail that never seemed to tire.

Terry's father pretended not to notice at first. "That dog," he'd say, whenever Magic trotted past his chair, as if the name itself were too much of an indulgence. But Magic had a way of working on a man — sitting at his feet during supper, curling up beside him when he read the paper, resting his chin on the old man's knee with a patience that asked nothing and offered everything.

One afternoon, when Terry stopped by with Eddie and the pup, his father opened the door before they could knock.

"Well," he grumbled, "bring that dog in before he scratches the paint."

Magic padded in like he owned the place. The old man reached down — not quite a pat, not quite an invitation — and Magic leaned into his hand as if he'd been waiting for that moment.

Later, as they were leaving, Terry's father cleared his throat.

"You know," he said, staring somewhere over Terry's shoulder, "if you ever need someone to watch that dog for a spell… well. I suppose he can come by. Anytime at all."

Eddie tried not to smile. Terry didn't bother hiding his.

Magic just wagged his tail, as if he'd known all along.

The Compass

As Terry was preparing to go to work, he noticed his new compass, the one he had recently ordered from Edmund Scientific, was missing.

He'd looked on his dresser to grab it — he liked carrying it in his pocket when he worked outside, a small reminder of the trails he meant to hike once spring settled in for good. He especially liked to fiddle with it on his lunch break. But the corner of the dresser where it always sat was bare.

He checked the top drawer. The nightstand. The workbench in the basement. His pockets.

Nothing.

"Eddie," he called, trying to keep his voice even, "you seen my compass?"

Eddie was sitting on the edge of his bed lacing his shoes. He froze for half a second — just long enough for Terry to notice.

"No, sir," Eddie said quickly. "I ain't touched it."

Terry studied him, but Eddie kept his eyes on his shoes. "All right," Terry said finally. "Maybe I misplaced it."

But the thought sat wrong in his gut.

A couple of days later, after stopping in Ramsey's Hardware to pick up a new drill bit, Terry found himself drifting toward the pawn shop. He hadn't planned on going in — not after the last time he'd seen Wally Harlan looking half-wild and unwashed — but curiosity tugged at him. Maybe Wally was ill. Maybe he'd been in a fight. Maybe Terry just wanted to know.

Inside, no Wally. A young woman sat behind the counter reading a book. She looked Asian, her dark hair neatly tied back, and she carried herself with the careful, slightly uncertain air of someone who hadn't been working there long.

"Where's Wally?" Terry asked.

She shrugged. "Don't know. He left town a few days ago. Didn't say where he was headed."

"When do you expect him back?"

"I don't think he'll be back. I hear the police are after him."

Terry nodded, taking that in, but not commenting.

As he was glancing around the shop, something had caught his eye — a small brass circle on the shelf behind the counter, sitting in plain view.

His compass.

The woman followed his gaze. "That? A boy brought it in two days back. Said he wanted to sell it."

Terry stepped closer. She handed it to him. "It's a very accurate compass, Edmund Scientific."

The markings were unmistakable —the clean shine of the brass, the needle steady and sure.

"How much?" he asked.

"Four dollars even."

Terry reached for his wallet and paid without another word.

That evening, Eddie was sitting on the back steps, elbows on his knees, staring at the yard like it might offer him a way out.

Terry stepped outside. "You want to tell me why you lied to me?"

Eddie's head jerked up. "I—I didn't—"

"Don't," Terry said sharply. "Not again."

Eddie swallowed hard. "I was just… I just wanted to look at it more. I didn't mean to keep it. Then I lost it. I swear I lost it. I was afraid to tell you."

"You didn't lose it," Terry said, anger rising like heat.

"You sold it!"

He pulled the compass from his pocket and held it close to Eddie's face.

Eddie flinched as if struck.

"I've been nothing but good to you," Terry shouted. "Clothes. Food. A place to stay. And you steal from me? Then lie about it?"

Eddie's eyes filled, but he said nothing.

"Go inside," Terry said. "I can't talk to you right now."

For the next three days, the house felt wrong. Not loud-wrong. Quiet-wrong.

Eddie kept to his room. Terry kept to his work. Meals were eaten in silence, the kind that settles heavy on a man's shoulders.

On the fourth afternoon, the phone rang. Terry was out back, so Eddie answered.

"Hello?"

"Eddie? Honey, is that you?"

It was Jeanie Whitmore, Jake's mother. Her voice was warm and tired in the way mothers' voices get when they've been tending a recovering child.

"Jake's been asking about you and Terry. He's lonely, stuck in the house recuperating. Would you two mind coming over for a visit, if you're not doing anything? Jake would really appreciate it."

Eddie hesitated. His throat tightened. "Yes, ma'am," he managed. "I'll tell Terry."

He stepped out onto the porch where Terry was tending his tomato plants.

"That was Jake's mom," Eddie said quietly. "She wants us to come by. Jake's lonely."

Terry paused, leaning on the rake handle. He didn't want to go — not with things the way they were — but he couldn't say no to Jake.

"All right," he said. "Let's go."

They drove in silence.

Jake was propped up on the living room couch, a blanket over his legs, a stack of comic books beside him. His face lit up when they walked in.

"Hey!" he said. "I was hoping you'd come."

Terry managed a smile. Eddie gave a small wave.

Terry pulled up a chair. "How you feeling, buddy?"

"Better," Jake said. "Still tired. Still sore. But better."

Terry nodded toward the sketchpad on the coffee table. "You been drawing any?"

Jake brightened a little. "Yeah. Mom says I gotta rest, but I've been doing at least thirty minutes a day. Helps the time go faster." He hesitated, then added, "It's not the same, though. Drawing's better when you've been out seeing things. Or talking to people."

Terry's smile softened. "I know what you mean."

Jake looked between them again, searching their faces. "What've you two been up to?"

"Not much," Terry said.

"Same," Eddie murmured.

Jake frowned. "You shown your drawing to anyone new?"

"Not yet," Terry said.

"You still driving that old truck?"

"Yeah."

"Been out on the river recently?"

"Just once," Terry said, a little too flat.

Jake's eyes narrowed. "Are y'all mad at me?"

Both of them startled.

"No," Terry said quickly.

"No," Eddie echoed.

Jake didn't buy it. Twelve-year-olds rarely do.

He studied them another moment, then asked quietly, "You mad at each other?"

Neither answered.

Jake shifted on the couch, wincing a little. "Me and Emmett had a big fight once," he said. "Didn't talk for a whole week. I thought he hated me. But he didn't. He was just waiting for me to say I was sorry. And I was waiting for him to say he was sorry."

He shrugged, simple and earnest. "Somebody's gotta go first. That's all."

Terry felt something in his chest loosen. Eddie stared at the floor.

They stayed another half hour, talking about the rummage sale and the campout Jake wished he could have attended. When they finally said goodbye, Jake gave them both a look that was far older than twelve.

The drive home was quiet, but not the same kind of quiet as before.

Halfway down Royal Avenue, Eddie spoke, barely above a whisper.

"I'm sorry, Terry."

Terry gripped the wheel, breathed once, and answered. "I'm sorry too. I shouldn't have yelled."

Eddie nodded, tears gathering but not falling. "I was stupid," he said.

"And I could say the same thing about myself, but neither of us is stupid. We both just made a mistake," Terry added.

Back home, Terry went to the dresser, took out the compass, and held it out.

"You can borrow it," he said. "But you ask first. That's how trust works."

Eddie took it carefully, reverently. "I will. I promise."

Terry rested a hand on his shoulder, then hesitated.

"Eddie… why'd you take it? Really. I need to understand."

Eddie's face tightened. He looked down at the compass in his hands, turning it once, twice, like he was trying to find the right words inside the brass.

"I don't know," he said finally. "I mean… I do, but I don't."

He swallowed hard.

"I liked how it felt. I liked holdin' it. And I wanted to look at it more. That part's true." A breath. "But then I got scared. I thought you'd be mad I took it without askin'. And once I got scared, I just… I went back to bein' the old me. The me from before."

He rubbed his hands together, frustrated with himself.

"That kid… he grabs things. Gets rid of 'em before anybody can yell. Doesn't think about nothin' but stoppin' the scared feeling." His voice cracked. "I wasn't thinkin' about you. I wasn't thinkin' at all. I just wanted the scared to stop. And then it was too late, and I didn't know how to fix it."

He finally looked up, eyes wet but steady.

"I ain't tryin' to be that kid anymore, Terry. I really ain't. But sometimes… sometimes he comes back before I can stop him."

Terry let out a slow breath, the kind that releases more than air.

"Thank you for telling me," he said quietly. "That's all I needed."

He squeezed Eddie's shoulder — light, steady.

"All right," he said. "We're good."

And they were. Not perfect. Not easy. But good — the kind of good that comes from something broken and mended, stronger at the seam.

The days that followed settled into a quieter rhythm. Eddie kept close to Magic, and Terry kept close to his work, but the sharp edge between them had softened. Something had shifted — not loudly, not all at once, but in the steady way trust grows back after being cracked. And just as the house found its balance again, the past — the deeper past — began to stir.

The Revelation

Whitmore had the ledger open on his desk when Terry and Eddie arrived at his office, the pages spread out beside a neat stack of typed sheets. The professor looked up, already drawing breath to greet him.

"Terry, good morning. The cryptologist —"

"Sorry, sir," Terry said quickly, shifting the framed drawing under his arm. "There's something I need to say first."

Whitmore paused, attentive.

Terry stepped closer and set the frame gently on the edge of the desk. "I've made up my mind about the drawing. I'd like to donate it to the state history museum. I've got some savings, and I don't need whatever money it might bring. And… well, I'd feel strange making a profit off it anyway."

Eddie shifted his weight, watching Terry with a kind of shy admiration he didn't quite know how to show.

For a moment Whitmore simply regarded him, the admiration plain in his expression. He rested a hand on the frame.

"That's a very generous and thoughtful decision, Terry. Truly. The museum will be honored to receive it. If you leave it with me, I'll see that the donation is handled properly and without delay."

He rose and carefully moved the drawing to a safe place leaning against the wall.

He began again, "The cryptologist finished," he said. "He provided a full word-for-word translation, but much of it is lists — names of séance participants, dates, household notes. Useful historically, but not… illuminating."

"So he has prepared a summary of the key entries. The ones that reveal Alethea's state of mind. Her purpose. Her guilt."

He slid the first page together with the small diary toward Terry.

"These are his words," Whitmore said. "Not mine. He labeled each section clearly."

Terry sat down and began to read.

Eddie stood behind Terry's chair, reading along in silence, his brow tightening as the story unfolded.

Cryptologist's Note: Overview

The book is part ledger and part diary. The ledger parts are records of séances conducted by Alethea, interspersed with personal reflections. The diary entries reveal a woman grieving deeply for her fiancé, Charles, who died in the war. She believed she bore responsibility for his death.

Entry — Early Spring, 1863

Charles has been gone these three months, and the house is too quiet. I walk from room to room and feel him everywhere and nowhere. I have folded my wedding dress away. I cannot bear to look at it.

The war drags on. I pray each night for it to end. I pray for the boys on both sides. I pray for Charles to come home, though I know he cannot.

Cryptologist's Note: The Plan

The following entries describe a system devised by Alethea and Charles before his death. She would observe enemy troop positions and encode the information in drawings resembling designs for needlework samplers. Vines represent rivers. Crossed vines represent the joining of the forks of the Shenandoah. X-marks represent groups of ten soldiers. She sent these drawings to Charles, believing she was helping hasten the end of the war.

Entry — Late Summer, 1863

I walked the ridge again today. The river below was bright as a blade. I counted the tents on the far bank. I marked them as we planned — ten to a cross. I traced the river's bend in vines. I stitched the joining of the forks.

I sent the drawing to Charles. I pray it reaches him swiftly. I pray it helps. I pray it ends this terrible fighting.

Entry — Two Weeks Later

He is gone.

They say the battle at the forks was fierce. They say the men fought like cornered animals. They say Charles fell early, struck down before the sun was high.

I have done this. I have brought him harm. I only wanted the war to end. I only wanted him home.

Cryptologist's Note: Séances

After Charles's death, Alethea conducted frequent séances. Many entries list participants and mundane details. The following are the most revealing.

Entry — Séance, November 1863

Charles spoke tonight. His voice was faint, like wind through a shutter, but I heard him.

He said it was not my fault. He said I acted out of love. He said I must let go.

But I cannot. The guilt sits in my chest like a stone. I carry it from room to room. I sleep with it. I wake with it.

Entry — Winter, 1864

I asked Charles whether I should repair the fence before the thaw. He said yes. I asked him whether I should plant beans this year. He said yes. I asked him whether he forgave me.

He said he never blamed me.

I do not know how to believe him.

Cryptologist's Note: Her Final Fear

Alethea expresses concern that her grave might be disturbed after her death — either because of her involvement in wartime intelligence or because of her spiritual practices. She makes arrangements accordingly.

Entry — Undated, likely late in life

I have made my decision. I will be buried in Prospect Hill Cemetery, in an unmarked grave. My grave stone will be placed in the family plot.

Let them remember me kindly, if they remember me at all. Let them leave my rest undisturbed.

Terry lowered the pages slowly.

Whitmore watched him, hands folded. "It's a tragic story," he said quietly. "But a human one. She wasn't a spy in the way people imagine. She was a young woman trying to end a war and bring her fiancé home. Unfortunately, her plan led to the death of her true love."

Terry nodded, still absorbing the weight of Alethea's words.

"She carried that guilt her whole life," he said.

"Yes," Whitmore replied. "And now, at last, we understand why."

Terry looked down at the diary again — the cramped handwriting written in code.

The truth had emerged.

And it was more heartbreaking, and more beautiful, than he had imagined.

"There's one more entry," Whitmore said. "The cryptologist translated it word for word. No summary this time. He thought it best to let it stand on its own."

He slid a single sheet toward Terry.

He began to read.

Entry — Undated (Final)

Last night I dreamed of the river.

I stood upon its bank, the water dark and smooth as glass. The air was still. I felt no fear.

A small boat came toward me, drifting without oars. In it sat a young man and a boy. I did not know them, yet they seemed familiar. They looked at me with kindness.

The young man held out his hand. I stepped into the boat. The river carried us without sound.

I felt no weight upon my chest. No stone. No sorrow. Only peace.

Charles was there also, though I did not see him. I felt his presence. He was glad for me.

When I woke, the house was quiet. I rose and opened the shutters. The morning light was soft upon the fields.

I think I am ready to rest.

Terry read the entry again, slower this time, letting the words settle. Halfway through, he stopped breathing.

The river. The boat. The young man and the boy.

He felt the hair rise on his arms. A shiver passed through him, sudden and thin, like the old saying about someone walking over your grave.

Whitmore waited quietly, hands folded on the desk, watching him with the patience of someone who had seen men encounter the past in unexpected ways.

Terry set the page down with great care. His voice, when it came, was low. "I had… that same dream."

Whitmore leaned forward surprised. "What?"

Terry nodded, unable to look away from the page. "Only… I was the young man in the boat."

A long silence opened between them — not frightening, just deep, like a well whose bottom you couldn't see.

Whitmore exhaled softly. "Some things echo," he said. "Across time, across grief. Sometimes across people."

Terry handed the paper back to Whitmore. "She carried so much," he murmured. "But she found her peace, looks like."

"It seems so," Whitmore agreed. Then he hesitated, choosing his words. "There's something else you should know."

Terry looked up.

"That drawing you found — the one right here," Whitmore said, pointing to Terry's drawing, "I believe it was the last one she ever made.

The one she sent to Charles." His voice softened. "The one that led to the battle where he was killed."

Terry felt the weight of that settle — not crushing, but solemn.

"She must have hidden it away," Whitmore continued. "Because she was ashamed, and the guilt was too much to bear."

Terry nodded slowly, absorbing it. The past no longer felt like a story. It felt like a hand laid gently on his shoulder.

"That's enough for today," he said quietly.

Whitmore gave a small nod. "Whenever you're interested in looking at some of the other materials I've recovered from the estate, you know where to find me."

He paused, his expression softening. "And Terry — thank you again for donating the drawing. It means more than you know."

Terry stood, feeling the weight of the past shift into something he could carry. He thanked Whitmore, stepped out into the hallway, and let the door ease shut behind him.

Eddie walked beside him a moment before speaking. "That was… something," he said. "I didn't know stories like that were real."

Terry looked at him, the boy who had carried so much of this story without knowing it. "Let's go home," he finally said.

Outside, the afternoon light was soft on the university lawns. Terry took a long breath, steady and quiet.

Nothing supernatural pressed on him — just the weight of a story finally understood.

The Recognition

In the fall of the year when the maples along the Shenandoah burned red and gold and the air carried that first clean bite of winter coming on, Terry Miller steered his new blue-and-white Chevy Bel Air south toward Richmond. The car rode smooth and sure beneath him, the kind of ride that made a man sit a little taller behind the wheel.

He wore his best suit and tie — the dark gray one Jeanette said made him look "respectable in all the right ways." Beside him, Jeanette Parker sat with her gloved hands folded neatly in her lap. Petite, red-haired, and steady-eyed, she had a way of looking at him that made him feel both seen and steadied. They had met at church in June, and without either of them naming it, something had taken root.

In the back seat, Eddie wore a suit and tie of his own. He kept tugging at the knot, then smoothing it again, as if unsure which gesture made him look more grown-up. His knee bounced with nervous energy.

"You think the Governor's really gonna be there?" he asked for the third time.

"That's what the letter said," Terry replied, keeping his eyes on the road. "But don't expect anything fancy. Probably just a handshake and a few words."

Eddie snorted softly. "A few words from the Governor is still a few words from the Governor."

The highway unspooled before them — fields rolling out in long, gentle waves, barns tucked into hollows, smoke rising from chimneys. It was the same Virginia Terry had always known, but today it felt different, as though the land itself were acknowledging something he hadn't quite let himself believe.

By early afternoon they reached the Virginia History Museum, a stately brick building with white columns and broad steps that reminded Terry of the high school back home. A small crowd had gathered near the entrance — reporters, museum staff, a few curious onlookers.

As Terry turned into the museum's parking lot, he slowed the car and let it idle for a moment. The building rose ahead of them — brick, white columns, the kind of place that made a man feel small and important at the same time. But Terry's hands tightened on the wheel.

Jeanette noticed. "You all right?"

He nodded, then shook his head. "I just wish…" He swallowed. "I wish Pops could've come. He'd have liked this. Or he would have, once."

Jeanette laid a gloved hand on his arm. "Terry, he'll still get to be part of it. Eddie's going to take pictures, remember? You can show them to Pops at home, where he's comfortable."

From the back seat, Eddie leaned forward, eager to be included. "Yeah! And I'm getting good at it too. Since you bought me this camera, I've been practicing. Even read a whole book about taking pictures." He tapped the case beside him. "And I've got a brand-new roll of Kodachrome film in here — thirty-six shots. I'm gonna get everything."

Terry turned slightly, looking at him. Eddie's face was bright, earnest, full of the kind of confidence Terry had never seen in him before.

"You'll do fine," Terry said quietly. "Your pictures will mean the world to him."

"They'll mean a lot to you too," Eddie said. "You'll see."

Jeanette smiled. "He's right, you know."

"If Pops was here, who would watch the dog?" Eddie asked. "We would've had to bring Magic too."

"Now, that would be a disaster," Terry chuckled.

He let out a slow breath, the tension easing from his shoulders. "All right," he said. "Let's go in."

And with that, he turned off the ignition, stepped out into the crisp fall air, and walked toward the museum with the two people who had become, in ways he was only beginning to understand, his family.

A man in a dark suit walked toward them.

"Mr. Miller? We're so glad you could come. The Governor will speak shortly."

Terry nodded, suddenly aware of the weight of the moment. Jeanette slipped her hand into his, warm and steady. Eddie hovered close behind, wide-eyed.

Inside, the ceremony was formal but not grand — the kind of event where people spoke with careful diction and stood a little straighter than usual. The drawing, now preserved under glass in an ornate frame, rested on an easel draped in blue cloth. It looked smaller than Terry remembered, but somehow more alive.

The Governor stepped to the podium.

"Today we honor Mr. Terry Miller of Front Royal," he began, "for his remarkable generosity in donating a rare nineteenth-century sampler design — a piece of Virginia's heritage that might easily have been lost. Thanks to his integrity and his willingness to place history above personal gain, this artifact will now be preserved for generations."

A murmur of approval moved through the room.

Terry felt his ears grow warm. He wasn't used to being looked at, much less applauded.

The Governor lifted a walnut plaque.

"For your contribution to the Commonwealth, we present you with this recognition of unselfish service."

Terry stepped forward. The applause rose around him — polite, sincere, and somehow overwhelming. He accepted the plaque, nodded once, and stepped back, wishing he knew where to put his hands.

Afterward, as people drifted toward the reception tables, Eddie nearly burst with excitement.

"You're a celebrity!" he said, eyes shining. "A real one!"

Terry shook his head, embarrassed. "Now, Eddie…"

"No," Eddie said, stepping closer, his voice fierce with conviction. "It's proof."

Terry looked at him. "Proof of what?"

"That you are a great man," Eddie said. "And now everyone knows it."

The words struck Terry harder than the applause had. He swallowed, unable to speak for a moment. Then he reached into his inside jacket pocket.

"Eddie," he said quietly, "I've got something for you."

He handed him a plain white envelope.

Eddie frowned, tore it open, and pulled out a single sheet of paper. His eyes moved across the page. Then he froze.

"Terry… this is…"

"It's my application," Terry said. "To adopt you. If you want that. If you're ready."

Eddie's breath hitched. His hands trembled.

"You mean… I'd be your son and you'd be my dad? For real?"

"For real," Terry said. "But only if you want it too."

Eddie looked up, his eyes bright and fierce with emotion he couldn't hide.

"Terry," he said, voice thick, "you're the best."

Outside, the autumn leaves rustled in the wind, bright as fire against the sky, as if the whole season were leaning in to celebrate the moment — the quiet, steady beginning of a new life.

Dedication

To the memory of the people of Front Royal who helped raise me, guide me, and steady my steps:

Laura Virginia Hale, Eleanor Norton, Bill Olinger, Bill Coffman,
Rev. Roscoe Johnson, Rice Matthews, E. Wilson Morrison, Eula Steed,
Dr. Elizabeth Sherman, Eva Thomas, Robert Wood, John Zunka,
Ted Bromfield, and my grandfather,
James Bennett — the "Green Hornet."

This book carries a piece of each of you.

www.ingramcontent.com/pod-product-compliance
Lightning Source LLC
LaVergne TN
LVHW100523110826
845146LV00002B/750

* 9 7 9 8 9 9 5 6 9 5 7 0 7 *